THE BREATH OF LIFE

Mastering the Breathing Techniques of Pranayama and Qi Gong

by George Ellis

Newcastle Publishing
North Hollywood, California

This book is not intended to diagnose, prescribe, or treat any ailment, nor is it intended in any way as a replacement for medical consultation when needed. The author and publisher of this book do not guarantee the efficacy of any of the methods herein described, and strongly suggest that at the first suspicion of any disease or disorder that the reader consult a physician.

Edited by Gina Misiroglu
Cover and interior design by Michele Lanci-Altomare

ISBN: 0-87877-183-2
A Newcastle book
First printing 1993
10 9 8 7 6 5 4 3 2 1
Printed in the United States of America.

Contents

Introduction

A person could, if he or she wished to, dedicate most of waking life to "keeping fit."

An early riser could begin the day with press-ups, weight lifting, aerobics, and a run, followed by a good rub down. A shower, a sauna, and a Jacuzzi, then a stint of transcendental meditation before breakfast (muesli, fruit juice, and decaffeinated coffee, of course) would ready him or her for a late morning cycle to work. An evening program of swimming, tennis, yoga, and a massage would amount to an ideal health routine for the modern, health-conscious individual. It is a pity that this leaves no time for getting on with the rest of one's life.

Can one, therefore, be audacious enough to propose yet another health technique to start the day with? That is what this book intends to do.

Pranayama and Qi Gong (pronounced "chee gong") have been practiced in India and in China respectively for over two thousand years. These breathing techniques have proved beneficial for generations of adepts. A part of yoga, Pranayama is the completion of its physical practices known as Hatha yoga; it is renowned for promoting physical and mental health. Qi Gong (or Chi Gong, the westernized spelling) means control (*Gong*) of *Qi* (material energy, or breath). Taoist, Buddhist, and Confucian schools all insist upon the control of Qi, for assuring a long and healthy life.

Both Pranayama and Qi Gong can be practiced with ease, in one's own home, at no expense. They are not time consuming. They are easy to learn and to practice. They are suitable for everyone: the young, the old, the healthy and the ill, the sedentary and the athletic. They promote a feeling of well-being. And they are novel. It is easier to keep up a new exercise in breath control than to repeat the same boring workout day after day. And finally, there's the psychological value of discovering how the body adapts to the influx of new energy.

Why, then, have these Oriental breathing techniques not achieved the popularity of Hatha yoga, meditation, or Tai Chi?[1] There are probably two reasons for this. The first is that breathing techniques are not as spectacular nor as immediately attractive to a novice as are the more obviously physical exercises. That was certainly the case with me. I underwent my first ten years of yoga and meditation while virtually ignoring Pranayama altogether. The second reason is simply a dearth of instructors.

There exists an Oriental myth that breathing techniques are dangerous in the hands of the uninitiated. They are supposed to bring about all sorts of miraculous powers such as levitation, mind reading, and psychokinensis; a risky business for your average taxi driver or bank clerk in the middle of his or her day's work. As a result, those who know do not tell, unless it is to proven disciples whose goal is nothing less than spiritual enlightenment. It used to be the case, therefore, that the only way that a person could learn about Pranayama or Qi Gong was to shave his or her head and renounce the world so as to join a Chinese monastic order or an Indian ashram.

In China, things are very different now. Dialectical Materialism during forty years of Communist rule has rid the country of many of its old beliefs. Traditions have been reexamined with a new scientific attitude. As a result, the valuable aspects of Qi Gong for health purposes have been studied and propagated. Experts now abound; from latter-day miracle workers to ordinary physical fitness instructors. Armies of early risers flood the parks and the squares of Chinese cities in order to put their teachings into practice. Outside of the martial arts, little of this is known in the West.

In India, too, something has changed in recent years. Largely responsible are the pioneering efforts of enlightened yogis such as Swami Kuvalayananda, founder of a Scientific Yoga Research Institute in Lonavla near Bombay in the 1930s (the name of the institute is one of those gloriously Indian mouthfuls, namely: the Kaivalyadhama-Shreeman Madhava Yoga-Mandira Samiti). Yoga, Ayurveda (traditional Indian medicine), and Pranayama are studied and practiced under controlled scientific conditions at the Lonavla Institute. Today, at Lonavla and elsewhere in India people like Dr. Garote, Dr. K. S. Joshi, and Swami Gitananda are training people from all walks of life and from all over the world to practice and themselves teach the technicalities of yoga and Pranayama.

It is therefore only now becoming possible to learn Indian breathing techniques from a competent teacher. A short handbook may help both to develop a more general interest in the public and to introduce some of the gentler breathing exercises to those who wish to practice.

A word of warning, before we start. Breathing techniques affect the lungs, the heart, and the brain. When practiced gently and in the specified manner, they promote fitness and health. If done too strenuously or assiduously, however, they can cause damage to each of these organs. There are also certain exercises that should not be practiced by people with specific ailments and pathological conditions. Throughout the book I shall point out any area of risk. I shall also continue to give gentle warnings as to the speed and force of practice. If you follow the simple instructions, Pranayama or Qi Gong will lead to lasting health and longevity. However, before you embark upon any exercise program, it is always best to consult your doctor, and evaluate your physical health. It's best to start off slowly, and increase exercise time as you become more comfortable with the exercises and techniques.

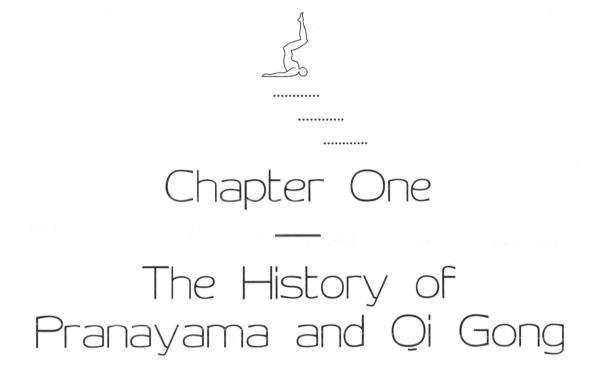

Chapter One

—

The History of Pranayama and Qi Gong

A fact which may have been clear to human beings since antiquity is the manifest connection between life and breath. Life depends on breathing, and breath, in most cultures, became synonymous with life, be it that of the deity, of the individual, or of the planet. Breath gives life, it surrounds one, is in one, is the most fundamental shared aspect of all living beings.

Those cultures that put greater store in the continuation of tradition and ideas sought to organize their theories of breath within the nascent philosophical systems and world views. Thus the Greeks, with their propensity for finding explanations within reality came up with the theory of Pneuma as a universal force in nature. The Indians, forever seeking the transcendence of the merely mundane, developed the theory of Prana: a semi-mystical force responsible for life, health, and enlightenment. The Chinese, always a more practical people preoccupied with eking out a living in a difficult environment, attempted to harness the essence of life in order to maintain health and extend personal survival indefinitely. These called the essence Qi.

Despite the different theoretical bases and being separated by the continental barrier of the Himalayas, in time the two great continuous cultures of Asia, the Indian and the Chinese, arrived at theories and practices of breath control for purely health purposes. The exercises that these two cultures developed are different, as are some of the ideas of physiology behind them. Nevertheless, the similarities are such and so many as to establish the universal validity of breath control exercises for the improvement and maintenance of health.

PRANAYAMA

Pranayama is a Sanskrit word meaning "a pause (*ayama*) of the breath (*Prana*)," or, more loosely, "breath control." It describes the various techniques of Indian yogic tradition that are aimed at disciplining the inhalation (*puraka*), retention (*kumbhaka*), and expiration (*rechaka*) of breath.

The concept that the control of a person's breathing might be of value to a long and healthy life probably derives from the Vedic identification of Prana with both the breath and the soul. The Vedas are a body of sacred hymns and oblational verses composed by the Aryans sometime between 1500 and 1200 B.C. The ancient Aryans observed that breath and life co-existed and that when one ceased, so did the other. The preservation of life would thus entail the preservation of breath. This would be attempted by breathing slowly or not at all for short periods. What lent conviction to these efforts was the belief, expressed in the Vedas and the Upanishads, that a person's life expectancy was to be measured not in years but in a specific number of breaths.

Medieval Yogic texts make reference to these beliefs in passages such as this one this from the definitive classical textbook on Hatha yoga, the fourteenth century A.D. *Hathapradipika*:

> *Even Brahma and the other gods devoted themselves to the practice of Pranayama as they feared death. Hence one should practice Pranayama.*

Or another from the text *Gorakshapaddhati*:

> *Due to fear of death even Brahma, the Lord of creation, keeps on practicing Pranayama, and so do many yogis and Munis. It is therefore recommended that a student of yoga always control his breath.*

The practice of Pranayama for purposes of longevity would no doubt have lead the ancient yogis to the discovery of other more immediate benefits. Their efforts at slowing their breathing to a near standstill must have revealed to them the direct link between respiration and the emotions. They could thus slow their heartbeat, control their feelings, and restrain a wayward mind. These effects would be of great practical value in the developing art of meditation that so interested the Indian psyche during the first millennium B.C.

What scholars do know with certainty is that by the second century B.C., Pranayama was regarded as an indispensable aid on the path toward spiritual enlightenment.

The Code of Manu (*Manu-Smrti*) dates, in its present form, from the first century B.C.; it is, however, based on a much earlier body of writing attributed to India's mythological first man: Manu. This text prescribes to the Hindu his *dharma*, or code of law, by which he or she must lead life as a member of one of the four social castes. Manu observes that Pranayama is a valid remedy against the evil tendencies that are inherent in the mind and the organs of sense (these are defined, by the way, as the tendencies of the mind to love and to hate, and of the senses to be attracted or repelled by external objects).

The most sacred of Indian texts, the second century B.C. *Bhagavadgita*, mentions Pranayama as a means toward spiritual enlightenment. When Lord Krishna explains the need to discard all attachment to external things in order to attain inner bliss and thus the beatitude of God, he says:

> *Shutting out all external objects and fixing his gaze between the eyebrows and making the inward and the outward breath equal in their course within the nostrils, the sage who is intent on liberation and has curbed his senses, mind and understanding, casting away all fear desire and anger —such a sage is delivered from all bondage.*[1]

It is, however, with Patanjali, the second century author of that yoga classic, the Yogasutras (or aphorisms on yoga), that the foundations of modern Pranayama techniques are laid. Patanjali's system of yoga follows eight stages on the way to the goal of *Samadhi*, or spiritual liberation. These stages are:

1) Self-restraint
2) Fixed observances (contentment, purity, austerity, self-study and self-surrender)
3) A suitable posture for meditating
4) The regulation of breath, or Pranayama
5) Abstraction
6) Concentration
7) Trance (*dhyana*)
8) Samadhi

Patanjali starts by defining yoga as "the inhibition of the modifications of the mind" so as to enable "the Seer to become established in his own essential and fundamental nature."[2] He continues to explain that:

The mind becomes clarified by cultivating attitudes of friendliness, compassion, gladness and indifference respectively toward happiness, misery, virtue and vice. Or by the expiration and retention of breath.[3]

Later, when he traces the steps that a yogi must take to achieve his end Patanjali states, in the section entitled Sadhana Pada, that once a comfortable posture has been mastered:

Pranayama, which is the cessation of inspiration and expiration, follows.

It is in external, internal or suppressed modification; it is regulated by place, time and number, and becomes progressively prolonged and subtle.

That Pranayama which goes beyond the sphere of internal and external is the fourth variety. From that is dissolved the covering of light. And the fitness of the mind for concentration is achieved.[4]

That is where classical yoga's greatest authority leaves us as far as Pranayama is concerned.

Tantric Pranayama

Patanjali's aphorisms were developed and expanded upon in the centuries that followed the development of Pranayama, although little has come down to us from sources earlier than the fourteenth century A.D. Nevertheless, there is evidence that Pranayama was practiced in a fairly advanced form from by adepts of Tantra. Tantra is a practical form of Hinduism which flourished in India between the sixth and twelfth centuries A.D. and which, in a more sophisticated guise, is still practiced to this day. Hindu Tantric thought holds that the supreme reality becomes manifest only through its inherent female energy or *Sakta*. The male personifications of the deity Brahma, Visnu, and Siva, for example, each manifest through their *Sakti*. Without her they are inert, as corpses. Tantra philosophy considers the macrocosm to be reflected within the microcosm of the human body. The female energy of the deity resides at the base of the spine as a coiled serpent, or *Kundalini*. The worship of Sakta entails the awakening of the Kundalini within the body. To this end a variety of unorthodox means were employed, the best known of these being ritual copulation between male and female adepts. It was here, in the copulation techniques, that Pranayama was practiced.

Tantric Pranayama served two purposes. The first was to harmonize the breath between the left and right nostrils. The left nostril was lunar and feminine, the right solar and masculine. The harmonization of breath between both partners would ensure a special ecstasy of cosmic proportions. The second purpose was to control male orgasm. Tantric couples were supposed to exchange their energies without any loss thereof due to ejaculation. Steady breathing was practiced in order to inhibit sexual passions, and, in particular, *kumbhaka,* or retention of breath was employed to hold back the surge of orgasm.

In the *Varahi Tantra* it is written:

> *The practitioner of Tantra aims at stopping the unconscious flow of micro-cosmic forces by achieving control of the functions of breathing, which represent the outward aspect of Prana. The initiate must master the breathing process until it becomes a most responsive and subtle tool.*

Hindu Tantrism was forced underground by the advent of Islam in the thirteenth and subsequent centuries. Mohammedan influence on native Indian culture was not, however, entirely detrimental. The alien ideas of Islam obliged the Hindus to take a closer look at themselves and at their by now fossilized religious traditions. The result was a Hindu renaissance that produced what are today considered to be the classical texts on Hatha yoga and Pranayama.

The Texts

The earliest of these is a text of uncertain date but probably medieval in origin called *Brihadyogiyajnavalkyasmrti*. This was written by a gentleman whose name appears in the middle of that mouthful, one Yajnavalkya. Actually the name only means "code of verses on yoga by Yajnavalkya." This author conforms to Patanjali's eightfold path of yoga in which Pranayama follows asanas, or postures, and precedes the meditative practices.

In his chapter on Pranayama, Yajnavalkya discusses various quaint means of measuring time during the practice of his breathing exercises. A "Matra," or basic unit of time, can, for instance, be measured either by: "Snapping the fingers thrice," "moving the hand around the knee once" or "clapping thrice."

A longer period called "Atimatra" is described as the time taken for "milking the cow, or cooking food, or shooting an arrow or ringing a bell."[5] One can only hope that precision in timing was not a requisite to successful practice.

Yajnavalkya goes on to discuss various methods of inhaling, retaining, exhaling with the repetition of *Mantras* (sacred syllables) and the reflection on the three deities: Visnu, Brahma, and Siva. The purpose, according to him, is to purify from sin. Thus:

> *With the combination of three factors, namely, Pranayama, reflection on three deities and the triad Agni, Vayu and Apa one is purified.*

> *Sixteen rounds of Pranayama when practiced daily for a month purify one even from the sin of killing an embryo.*

> *Just as the impurities of metal are burnt after being blown by fire, similarly the abnormalities of the organs are removed by controlling Prana.*

> *For the purification of sin caused by unknowingly killing insects day and night, six Pranayamas should be practiced methodically after bath.*[6]

Even more heinous crimes than these can be removed through assiduous practice:

> *A murderer of a Brahmin, a drinker of liquor, a debaucher, a robber of gold, a thief, a person noxious to kith and kin, a treacherous person, a killer of a refugee, a false witness, one engaged in evil deeds, all these and others engaged in sinful acts for a long time reach sacred Svarga (Heaven) like those persons doing good deeds, if they practice hundred Pranayamas at the sunrise.*[7]

The views of later writers on the benefits of Pranayama are more concerned with health.

According to Svatmarama, the author of the *Hathapradipika* compiled sometime between 1350 and 1550, Pranayama serves to purify the nadis which are any organs in the body that function as a passage for the transmission of food, drink, blood, lymph, or nervous impulse. He does, however, also assert that:

> *The Yogi who, sitting in the Padmasana (pose), holds the air inhaled through the nostrils is surely to be liberated. There is no doubt about it.*[8]

Hatha yoga, under which heading Svatmarama places the practice of Pranayama, is of value, in his view, only if it aims at spiritual liberation. To this end he describes suitable physical exercises, cleansing techniques, diet, and eight varieties of Pranayama which to this day constitute the foundation of Hatha yoga. When, later in the book, we look at various exercises in Pranayama, we shall make ample reference to Svatmarama's classic text.

Other texts that we shall refer to are the sixteenth century *Astanga Yoga* by Swami Charandasa and the *Gheranda Samhita*, which is presented as a dialogue between Gheranda, who probably lived in the second half of the seventeenth century, and his disciple, Candakapali.

The Tradition

The theme running through all these works is the final goal of Samadhi. According to them, the practice of yoga techniques for their own sake is fruitless.

This is a view that held sway in India until the second decade of this century. Pranayama was regarded as a strictly spiritual discipline, the secrets of which were to be divulged to no one outside an elect circle of advanced yogis. The powers inherent in the practice of Pranayama were supposedly too great to be allowed into the hands of the uninitiated. When, however, Pranayama began to be the focus of laboratory investigation in the 1920s and 1930s, those powers proved to be wholly imaginary. No one performing Pranayama has ever been observed to leave his or her body or to levitate or to carry off feats of telepathy or clairvoyance. At the very worst, a person may bring upon him- or herself a little dizziness from hyperoxygenation, or develop a larger appetite than usual. On the other hand, the systematic observation of Pranayama practitioners has revealed unsuspected medical benefits inherent in many of the techniques.

Pranayama has been practiced for health reasons since the 1950s in yoga institutes in India and abroad, and teachers have been trained in modern therapeutic methods. Nonetheless, Pranayama remains a much misunderstood practice which is all too often shrouded in mystery. The words that Professor Joseph Needham wrote in 1956 in *Science and Civilization in China* when he discussed Pranayama still hold true today:

> *The facts concerning Indian Yogism are very hard to get at, since the practices have always been transmitted personally from guru to disciple, and outsiders have to approach them through a haze of uncritical mystification.*[9]

In the nearly forty years that have elapsed since Professor Needham wrote these words above, yoga has become perhaps more popular in the West than in its native India. Yoga instructors abound in all shapes and sizes; books on the subject can be purchased on any station and airport bookstall in virtually every Western nation. Nevertheless, Pranayama, the fourth limb of Patanjali's ancient system, remains, to most people's minds, an esoteric and dangerous practice best left to long-haired ascetics sitting cross-legged in Himalayan caves.

I hope, in the pages that follow, to contribute in some small measure to ending this time-worn myth.

QI GONG

If Indian Pranayama is little know in the West, Qi Gong is even less so. Most people have at least heard of Pranayama, few have of its Chinese counterpart. This is true despite the fact that the martial arts which evolved directly from Qi Gong have achieved great popularity in recent years.

Qi (pronounced "Chee") corresponds to the Sanskrit "Prana." It means breath, or breath of life. It also means material energy, vital matter, life force, the earth's atmosphere, or the fundamental substance of material beings. Gong (pronounced "gong") means mental control over the body. Qi Gong thus means mental control over the flow of Qi in one's body. In the oldest extant reference to Qi Gong by the philosopher Guan Zi, who lived during the Warring States Period (476-221 B.C.), it is defined as a method of dealing with the spirit.

The origins of Qi Gong are said, however, to be more ancient. There exists pictorial evidence from Shang and Zhou dynasty bronzes (1122-770 B.C.) that Qi Gong breathing exercises were then being used for medical purposes. It was probably noticed, in prehistoric times, that involuntary breaks in the rhythm of breathing, like yawning or groaning, brought some relief to tiredness and pain. It followed, therefore, that if one were to regulate the depth and speed of one's breathing voluntarily, one might alleviate many of the symptoms of ill-health.

These early practices became part of the empirical tradition of Chinese medicine. Breathing techniques were used, within this tradition, for both curative and preventive purposes. The anonymous *Huang-Di Nei-Jing*, the Han or possibly Qin dynasty (sometime between 221 B.C. and 220 A.D.) canon of Chinese internal medicine, states in *Pure Questions, Inner Classic of the Yellow Emperor*:

> *The cause of disease lies chiefly in the malfunctioning of the circulation of Qi. The Qi in external forces, for example wind, cold, heat, and humidity, penetrates the body's internal organs*

and causes disease. Internally, the disturbance of the circulation of Qi through the five "zang" [the heart, liver, spleen, lungs, and kidneys] and the six "fu" [gallbladder, stomach, large and small intestines, bladder, and imaginary organ by the name of "san-qiao" [or three body cavities] is also a cause of disease.

Hence the need for Qi Gong to put things right. The same text prescribes that:

One must breathe the essence of life, regulate one's respiration to preserve one's spirit and keep the muscles relaxed.

Or, again, that:

Those with kidney trouble may do the following exercises in order to cure the disease: stand with the face turned toward the south in the early morning and breathe in seven times without thinking of anything.[10]

A tomb in Changsha in Hunan Province, dating from the Western Han dynasty (206 B.C. to 24 A.D.) provides pictorial evidence of the practice of Qi Gong. Forty-four pieces of colored silk found in this tomb depict people of all ages performing exercises that imitate the movements of the tiger, deer, bear, ape, and bird. Next to one of the figures, are the words, "Look toward the sky and exhale."

The maintenance of a proper flow of Qi within the body was the subject matter of several books which appeared in the first centuries of the Christian era. One called *Nan Jing* (a classic on disorders) by a doctor, Bian Que, describes how to keep one's Qi flowing through the use of breathing techniques and acupuncture. During the Jin dynasty (265-420 A.D.) another physician, Hua Tuo, began using acupuncture for anesthesia in surgery. He also promoted the Taoist Wu Qing Xi (Five Animal Sport) exercises, as found in the Changsha tomb, to generate local Qi circulation.

Many of the physicians who were exploring the functions of the human body were Taoists, Confucians, or Buddhists. It was thus inevitable that their studies should be influenced by the wider philosophical systems in which they believed. The following centuries thus saw the development of different schools of Qi Gong. They were that of the Taoist, the Confucian, the Buddhist, and the Martial Arts.

The everyday Chinese world view ceased to make any clear distinction between its three major religious philosophies long ago. Nevertheless, the different goals of these philosophical systems have left their mark on the Qi Gong practiced in China today. In order, therefore, to understand the place of Qi Gong breathing techniques within modern Chinese culture and medicine, it is beneficial to look at their development within each of the major religious-philosophical systems in turn.

Qi Gong and Taoism

According to legend, Taoism was founded by a man known as Lao Tzu in the sixth century B.C. Actually, this traditional birth really only marks somebody's attempt to make sense of the animistic Shamanism and nature worship that came before. Lao Tzu himself is said to have been born already old and wise in about 600 B.C. but it might have been two centuries later, after gestating for eighty-two years in his unfortunate mother's womb. At the end of his life, during which, according to one story, he had been keeper of the imperial archives in Luoyang, Lao Tzu grew sick at heart of the ways of men and set off toward the West sitting on the back of a water buffalo. Before leaving the civilized world, that is China, he was asked by a gatekeeper at the frontier to record his beliefs for posterity. This he condescended to do. The result was a five-thousand-character volume called *Tao Te Ching*, or *The Way and its Power*. That is all that is known about him; even his name, Lao Tzu, only means Old Master. The *Tao Te Ching* is, however, without a doubt China's outstanding contribution to world literature. Its message of gentle transcendence over human affairs holds a universal and lasting appeal and represents the pinnacle of Taoist thought.

Mystic philosophy is not, however, all that Taoism is about. It is also made up of a mixture of superstitions, exercises, and metaphysical concepts within which we find an elaborate theory of Qi Gong.

Taoist Qi Gong originated as a purification exercise aiming at nothing less than material immortality. An impure Qi, to be understood here as "material energy," was regarded as the cause of decadence and death. If the Qi were suitably cleansed, a human being would become a "Xian," or true immortal. The necessary cleansing techniques consisted of physical exercises, sunbathing, sexual union, the use of herbal and alchemical preparations, a vegetarian diet, and Qi Gong breathing.

A belief that developed quite early in Taoism was that, before birth, the human embryo existed in a sort of uncontaminated vacuum within the mother's womb. To return to this breathless condition would mean to achieve the perfection that lead to immortality. Budding Xians would thus dedicate much of their time to holding their breath (Pi Qi). The resulting cold sweat and dizziness were probably held to be intimations of immortality.

How it was done is suggested by the inscription found on a sixth century B.C. jade handle of a staff described by the German sinologist, H. Wilhelm, in 1930. It reads:

In breathing one must proceed [as follows]. One holds [the breath] and it is collected together. If it is collected, it expands. When it expands, it goes down. When it goes down it becomes quiet. When it becomes quiet it will solidify. When it becomes solidified it will begin to sprout. After it has sprouted it will grow. As it grows it will be pulled back again [to the upper regions]. When it has been pulled back it will reach the crown of the head. Above, it will press against the crown of the head. Below, it will press downward.

Whoever follows this will live; whoever acts contrary to this will die.[11]

Over twelve centuries later, Tang dynasty Taoists (618-907 A.D.) were still chasing the same dream. They stretched and massaged, men sunbathed and women moonbathed in the nude, they ate vegetarian diets so as not to contaminate themselves with the Qi in the blood of animals, and they held their breath. They had, however, stopped copulating in public because of complaints from their more prudish Confucian and Buddhist neighbors. Apart from this, only the techniques had evolved slightly.

Ordinary respiration, Wai Dan, had been replaced by an inner respiration called Nei Dan. "Ordinary people breathe through the throat but the saint breathes through the whole body, starting from the heels," had asserted Zhuang-zi in about the second century B.C. Tang dynasty Taoists took this to heart. They regarded the inner breath as human's share of primordial life. They regulated the flow of Qi within the body by means of an inwardly turned meditative vision of the eyes. In the case of sickness, they attempted to direct this healing flow to the seat of the disease.

Men also mixed their internal Qi with semen. It was supposed to rejuvenate the organs and kill off the three worms (San Chong) that were held responsible for aging. An ancient Chinese saying went:

Heaven has three treasures
They are the sun, the moon and the stars.
The earth has three treasures.
They are water, fire and wind.
Man has three treasures.
They are semen (Jing), breath (Qi) and spirit (Shen).[12]

The technique was simple. One pressed hard on the urethra, between the anus and the scrotum, at the moment of ejaculation. This was supposed to suck the Jing back into the body where it mixed with the Qi. In actual fact, this technique only sends the semen into the bladder from where it is eliminated with the urine. The Taoists, however, did not know this.

It may appear from all this that Taoist Qi Gong was based on such confused notions of physiology as to be quite useless to anyone interested in their breathing exercises for less fantastic purposes than achieving immortality. However, despite these notions, centuries of trial and error have, in the end, produced a good deal of value. The health benefits which Taoist practices were genuinely able to produce have survived the test of time. They were filtered into traditional Chinese medicine, and it is in this guise that they have come down to us today.

Qi Gong and Confucianism

The Confucians and the Taoists were always archrivals.

"Irresponsible hermits," accused the Confucians.

"Pedantic literati," countered the Taoists.

Confucians loved form and artifice, Taoists spontaneity. Confucians believed in an ideal society based on the gentlemanly virtues of obedience to tradition, and to authority. The Taoists didn't believe in society at all.

Despite their differences, Confucians and Taoists never really fell out with one another completely. They simply each accepted the separate domain of the other's philosophy, and steered clear of confrontations. This resulted in the growth of two independent schools of thought which cater for the Chinese propensity for both metaphysics and practicality.

Confucius (Khung Fu Tzu, or Master Khung) was born in the small state of Lu, in what is now Shandong Province, in 552 B.C. They were turbulent times. After the end of the mythical Golden Age of the Zhou dynasty in 771 B.C., China was divided into hundreds of small princely states fighting it out for survival or for dominance over their neighbors. According to Confucius, peace and prosperity would be restored to society only if the values and traditions of the "Golden Age of Zhou" were used as a model.

Confucius thus spent most of his life offering local warlords unsolicited advice on how to go about this. He died at the age of seventy-two without ever having been listened to. Nevertheless, within a century of his death, Confucius' ideas had taken root. They became the theoretical base for all political and social thinking in China until their partial eclipse with the advent of Communism.

Confucianism required that a peaceful society be based on order and harmony. It emphasized the need to respect human dignity. Interpersonal relationships were clearly defined in terms of duties and rituals that had to be followed. And the Confucian gentleman cultivated courtesy, selflessness, and moderation in all his actions. When he ate, or sipped tea, he would do so harmoniously. He never hurried or ran or raised his voice unless it was for some purely altruistic motive. If he played or listened to music, if he recited poetry, or if he painted a picture, it was solely for the sake of introspection and self-improvement. Even his breathing was calm, slow, and composed.

Confucian Qi Gong, therefore, served the general purpose of self-betterment. By controlling his breath the Confucian was able to control his feelings, moods, and actions, and to improve himself as a consequence.

When that great Confucian philosopher Mencius (Meng-Tzu), who lived from 371-289 B.C., was asked the reason for his superiority over ordinary men, he replied: "I know how to nourish my vast flowing Qi."

According to Mencius, only when the Qi in a person is fully developed do the decree of heaven and the will of man become one.

This kind of metaphysics, however, played only a marginal role in Confucianism until the increased influence of Buddhism, during the third to the ninth century A.D., obliged the Confucians to provide a theological foundation for their social theories. Neo-Confucianism resulted in the eleventh century as a synthesis of the transcendental and the mundane in Chinese philosophy. With this synthesis, Taoist and Tantric Buddhist ideas of Qi and Qi Gong made their way into Confucianism, too. From the eleventh century onward, therefore, the theory and practice of Taoist, Tantric, and Confucian Qi Gong are thoroughly intertwined.

Qi Gong and Buddhism

Buddhism came to China from India in fits and starts between the second and fifth centuries A.D. Its founder, Gautama Siddharta, Prince of the Sakya clan, was born in what is now southern Nepal in 563 B.C. He achieved "Enlightenment," or Buddhahood, at the age of about thirty-five and spent the rest of his long life (he died of mushroom poisoning at eighty-one years of age) preaching to a small band of disciples.

Buddha was really only one of the many reformers to breathe new life into the excessively ritualistic Hinduism of the time; he probably taught a practical form of yoga that shied away from metaphysics and devotional practices. Only when the Mauryan Emperor Ashoka adopted Buddhism as his personal creed, in about 270 B.C., did Buddhism emerge as a distinct religion. Ashoka's contribution was to found a rule of Dharma ("according to Buddhist doctrine") at home, and to send monks abroad to spread the message of the new creed.

Buddhism's introduction into China began during the Han dynasties (206 B.C. to 220 A.D.). Chinese travelers visiting the Buddhist states of central Asia were the first to bring home notions of the new religion. Cultural and trade exchanges with India were common at that time and continued until well into the Tang dynasty (618-907 A.D.). During this period, cultured elite who were enamored neither of Taoist superstition, nor of Confucian formalism, adopted Buddhism as their creed.

Buddhism, with its foreign concepts of reincarnation, maya (the illusory nature of the world), karma, and personal enlightenment never won universal acceptance in China. Temples were built, and so were monasteries, but there were also occasions when they were destroyed. Two schools of Chinese Buddhism did, however, take root. One was the Chan school of world-renouncing meditation founded by the Indian monk Bodhidharma or Da Mo who died in China in the sixth century A.D. The other was Tantric Buddhism which may have been imported from India in the eighth century.[13]

Chan and Tantra are the yin and yang of Buddhism: the two opposites co-existing in the same religion. Chan, which, incidentally, comes from Dhyana (or the Sanskrit "meditation") and which in Japanese is pronounced "Zen" is a life-denying, thoroughly ascetic path to enlightenment. Tantra, on the other hand, indulged in life. Despite their differences, both schools employed breathing techniques as part of their practice.

Tantric Buddhism: Tantric Buddhism, also referred to as Vajrayana, was taken from India to neighboring Tibet and southwestern China by an Indian magician and charismatic holy man called Padmasambhava—though also known as Guru Rimpoche—in the eighth century A.D. Based on complex symbolism and ritual, Tantric Buddhism promoted the use of breath control for the same purposes as did the Hindu Tantras. The idea was to exchange male and female breaths during ritual copulation. According to ancient Tibetan Vajrayana parchments, the respiratory technique was supposed to exercise such control over the sex act "in such a manner that the semen goes its way backward, not descending but ascending, till it reaches the 'thousand-petalled lotus' at the top of the head."[14] The "thousand-petalled lotus" at the top of the head is, by the way, the seat of enlightenment according to Tantric theory.

At the same time, Qi Gong was used by Buddhists to control breathing and internal energy and, as a consequence, orgasm. More about that later, however.

Chan Buddhism: When Bodhidharma arrived in China in about 526 A.D., he went first to Canton. There he was granted audience by the Emperor Wu Ti, but failed to convince the great man of the validity of his life-renouncing form of

Buddhism. Bodhidharma subsequently traveled to the monastery of Shaolin in Henan Province where he spent the rest of his life and adopted the Chinese name of Da Mo.

When he first arrived in Shaolin, Bodhidharma, or Da Mo, was taken aback by the emaciated condition of the monks living there. His initial reaction was to meditate. This he did for nine long years during which he trained other monks in the art of Chan meditation and Pranayama. He also wrote two books. One of these, called *Yi Jin Jing (The Book of Muscle Development)* prescribed a series of exercises for ensuring the physical fitness of the Shaolin monks.

The *Yi Jin Jing*'s exercises aimed at circulating and building up internal Qi by means of both Wai Dan (external) breathing with specific movements and postures, and Nei Dan (internal) breathing with meditation. Nei Dan was based on ordinary yogic meditation, but was used here, not as a spiritual technique, but to counteract the dispersive effects of the Wai Dan movements. Wai Dan, itself, was a novel technique for concentrating Qi in various muscles used in the martial arts. Over the following 1,400 years it evolved to become the world-renowned Shaolin martial arts technique of Gong Fu, or, as it is more commonly known, Kung Fu, or the Art of Control.

Before we look at the martial arts we might consider the question of origin. Could Qi Gong have originated from Pranayama or did the latter, perhaps, derive from Qi Gong?

The two theories are sufficiently similar to make this question quite legitimate. Both cultures regard Prana, or Qi, as life energy. Both India and China equated life energy with breath. And in both countries techniques were developed for controlling breathing.

However, we have already noted that India and China both trace their theories on breath to ancient and wholly local sources. We might speculate about whether there could have been some common prehistoric seed to both systems. One could quite reasonably argue in favor of a central Asian origin, throwing in the Greek theory of Pneuma in too for good measure. This is pure speculation, however. As far as we are concerned, we can safely assume that apart from the direct link between Indian Pranayama and Bodhidharma's Chan Qi Gong, the Chinese and Indian systems developed along sufficiently different paths as to constitute two independent theories.

Pranayama was interested, until recently, only in spiritual awakening. Qi Gong aimed toward the steady circulation of energy, to health and to immortality. Pranayama was always practiced in the yogic cross-legged Lotus posture, while many Qi Gong exercises entail movement. Finally, Qi Gong is, today, in China, a frequently practiced exercise about which a great deal is known to lay people.

Pranayama is still considered an esoteric art to be handed down personally from guru to disciple.

Qi Gong and the Martial Arts

The monks of Shaolin monastery were obliged to defend themselves against brigands who used to attack them both in the monastery itself and on journeys through the countryside. They therefore developed Bodhidharma's original fitness exercises into a series of techniques for self-defense. These techniques were named after animals well-known for their fighting prowess: the tiger, the leopard, the dragon, the snake, and the crane. It is by these names that Shaolin Gong Fu styles are still known today.

The fighting abilities of the Shaolin monks became legendary. At the beginning of the Tang dynasty (618-907 A.D.), thirteen monks had single-handedly rescued the Emperor Tai Zong from a rebel army. During the sixteenth century, Shaolin monks were employed to rid China's eastern coasts of Japanese pirates.

As a consequence of this prowess, other schools of martial arts grew up in China. During the Song dynasty (960-1279 A.D.), one Zhang San Feng created a martial form of Nei Dan Qi Gong called Tai Ji Quan. In this now well-known system, internal energy is built up from an area in the lower abdomen and circulated through the body for use in combat.

During the Southern Song Dynasty a famous general and patriot, Yue Fei, modified Bodhidharma's original exercises in order to train his troops. This system came to be called Ba Duan Jin, or "Eight Pieces of Brocade." Yue Fei is also credited with the invention of the Qi Gong rapid punching technique known as Xing Yi. Also from this period is the Liu He Ba Fa technique invented by a hermit on Mount Hua. In this system, the body combines and coordinates with the mind, which combines with an idea, which combines with Qi, which combines with the spirit, which combines with movements, which combine and coordinate with the universe. To do it, a person concentrates on breathing.

Later martial Qi Gong systems that have survived to this day are the Ming Dynasty Huo Long Gong (Fire Dragon Control) technique created in about 1640, and Ba Gua Quan invented in Beijing between 1866 and 1880.

Most of these techniques were known, until quite recently, only to select groups of people: Buddhist monks or single families. Tai Ji Quan, for example, used to be a closely guarded secret of the Chen family until the middle of the nineteenth century. It was only when Chen Chang Xian the grand master at that time, taught the system to one Yang Lu Shan who passed it on to his sons who finally made it public, that Tai Ji Quan became known at all.

Shaolin Wai Dan was first taught outside the Chan monastic order in the 1940s. A Shaolin Boxing Union was set up in Japan in 1946 to teach some of the techniques abroad, but it was really only in 1988 that a true international school for teaching Shaolin Wu Shu (the more usual Chinese name for Gong Fu) was set up in China.

The promulgation of the martial arts coincided with the introduction into China of Western ideas, particularly of Western science, during the first decades of the twentieth century. Westernization brought critical research to bear on the martial arts and on Qi Gong. All unscientific and superstitious aspects of the practices were consequently discarded. What remained were the health and fitness techniques which deserved further study and, eventually, general publicity.

Qi Gong Today

After the foundation of the People's Republic of China in 1949, the Communist government took a new interest in China's cultural heritage and in Qi Gong in particular. To begin with a few research institutes and sanitariums were set up around the country, only to be disbanded when China turned its back on its past during the cultural revolution (1966-1976). Interest in Qi Gong picked up again, however, after 1976. The Beijing Qi Gong Institute was established in December 1979. Exercises such as the eight and the twelve brocade techniques (Ba Duan Jin and Shi Er Duan Jin), Tai Ji Quan, Ba Gua Quan, and other martial Qi Gong systems are taught in city parks, hotels, schools, and offices. Nei Dan therapeutic breathing is performed in nearly every home. Qi Gong has, furthermore, been used by medical professionals to treat high blood pressure, neuroses, and some tumors, and, for many patients, it has proved to be an efficient anesthetic.

Scientific research on Qi Gong naturally ignored the quainter notions that derived from Taoism and Confucianism. Nevertheless, the fundamental concept that every living organism depends for its efficiency on the proper circulation of Qi is too deeply ingrained in the Chinese psyche to be discarded by any but the most rabid skeptics. When the body falls ill or begins to slow down with age, most people in China turn naturally to the gentle energizing techniques of Wai Dan or Nei Dan Qi Gong.

Qi Gong has, in fact, become so popular in recent years that the Chinese government has begun to express some concern about its uncontrolled proliferation. Although encouraged at first by Party elders, Qi Gong is becoming too popular for its own good. Too many quacks are setting up shop as miracle healers, claiming cures even at a distance. Furthermore, after June 1989, the government has been concerned about the threat to political stability inherent in allowing too much freedom to large groups and popular organizations. Qi Gong would seem to be so popular as to constitute a threat, in the authorities' eyes, to the government's control over Chinese society. This is despite the fact that China's gerontocracy itself keeps fit, healthy, and in power by means of the assiduous practice of Qi Gong.

············

············

············

Chapter Two

—

A Comparison of Pranayama and Qi Gong

Both Pranayama and Qi Gong purport to arrive at physical and spiritual well-being through the control of breathing. Theories concerning the nature of Qi and Prana have many points in common, and some of the techniques employed by Qi Gong and Pranayama are the same. Despite the similarities, however, Pranayama and the various schools of Qi Gong belong, as we have just seen, to very different cultural and historical traditions. Some fundamental differences in theory and practice are therefore inevitable.

The prospective student of Oriental breathing techniques is faced with a choice that he or she cannot adequately make unless he or she understands what the differences between Pranayama and Qi Gong really are.

At first glance, Pranayama might appear to be a more passive exercise than Qi Gong. Pranayama is performed exclusively in the seated or the standing position, while Qi Gong can entail a good deal of physical movement as well. Pranayama would thus seem the ideal exercise for the lazy person, and Qi Gong for the more active. However, if we examine the two systems a little more closely, we realize that this distinction is a gross simplification. Pranayama and Hatha yoga exist within the wider tradition of Hatha yoga which entails as much, if not more, movement than does Qi Gong. Strictly speaking we should thus be comparing Pranayama to the Nei Dan techniques of Qi Gong, and the asanas (postures) of Hatha Yoga to Wai Dan.

On both these scores, Indian yoga seems to offer a greater variety of techniques. Qi Gong's Nei Dan breathing is, for example, the same as the simpler techniques of Pranayama, but Pranayama develops these and perfects at least a dozen variations on the basic theme, each of which serve some specific therapeutic or "spiritual" purpose. Hatha yoga has developed hundreds of asanas which undeniably give more variety of physical exercise than do the dozen or so techniques of Wai Dan.

Qi Gong appears to place greater emphasis on the accumulation and flow of energy within the body, and has developed schools of martial arts that do not exist in India. Qi flow for therapeutic purposes is common in China. In India, on the other hand, it is virtually unknown apart from in the practice of Tantric yoga. The Tantric theory of the Kundalini serpent-power rising through the *Chakras*, or energy centers of the body, closely resembles the Chinese theory of internal Qi giving energy to the whole body. Tantrics regulate and concentrate the flow of Prana along various channels within the body in much the same way as Qi Gong masters describe.

Individual requirements differ and the best way to discover your own preferences in the way of breathing exercises is to try them all. You may, in this manner, form at least a tentative impression of what feels good and what doesn't. You will, in addition, find valuable information about the proven benefits of each technique where these are described in the practice section of this book.

Care must be taken, however, not to jump around too much from one exercise to another. Find the exercises you prefer, on the basis of both your personal sensations and the specified benefits, and keep at them.

The Indian sage, Ramakrishna, once said when talking about perseverance in yoga, that if you are digging a well, you continue digging until you find water. You don't dig half a well in a dozen places, thus wasting your time and energy altogether. Or, as the Chinese say in reference to Qi Gong: "A hundred days of practice lead to a single step of progress. A thousand days lead to a thousand steps."

THE BENEFITS OF PRANAYAMA AND QI GONG

Perhaps the most important question to ask is: "What can Pranayama and Qi Gong do for me?"

Traditionally, as we have seen, breathing techniques were developed within the framework of established schools of philosophy. They were no more than means to "higher ends" such as material immortality, spiritual transcendence, or a Confucian utopia. Pranayama continues to be practiced to this day for purely spiritual purposes, and Qi Gong is still regarded in China as a method for awakening and controlling the curative powers of the Qi.

Not everyone in the West will feel that these aims are exactly what we are all striving for. Therefore, while we can admit that slow, deep breathing can do a world of good to someone bent on achieving Samadhi, most of us will require more mundane reasons for taking any interest in Oriental breathing techniques.

The value of an exercise, for the majority of us, depends on its capacity to confer health: to prevent and to cure illness. Sufficient evidence exists to show that Pranayama and Qi Gong can do this. Good health depends on the correct functioning of the respiratory, the nervous, the endocrine, the digestive, and the circulatory systems of the body. The breathing techniques that are practiced today in the East have been shown, in the laboratory, to exert a beneficial effect on all these functions.

Oxygen is, of course, indispensable to life. It is carried in the blood to every cell and tissue in the body, and, through the process of oxidization, it liberates the energy stored within molecules in the body. Without an adequate supply of oxygen the cells are starved of the energy necessary to continue living. Pranayama and Qi Gong exercises work specifically toward ensuring a rich supply of oxygen to the lungs and hence to the blood and the cells. That may sound fairly obvious; breathing exercises are supposed to increase oxygen intake, are they not? However, it is not as simple as that. In actual fact, during the practice of Pranayama and Nei Dan Qi Gong, the consumption of oxygen decreases. The average person absorbs about fourteen pints (seven liters) of air during one minute of normal breathing. The same person will inhale not more than seven pints (three and a half liters) while engaged in Pranayama with breath retention. Furthermore, it has been shown experimentally—at the Kaivalyadhama Institute in Lonavla, India—that the absorption of oxygen is not affected by the time air is retained in the lungs.

Wherein, therefore, the enrichment of the oxygen supply to the cells brought about by breathing techniques? The answer lies simply in the training that Qi Gong and Pranayama give the respiratory system as a whole. It is not a few minutes of exercise that matters, as far as oxygen absorption is concerned, but efficient respiration during the rest of the day. Good breathing depends on powerful respiratory muscles and on the elasticity of the lungs. Pranayama and Qi Gong work toward ensuring these.

Breathing exercises tone up the respiratory system, and, as a consequence, the nervous and endocrine systems that are dependent upon the quality of the blood. They also help the organs of digestion to function properly. These are in the abdomen, below the lungs. Pulmonary movements therefore normally exert a gentle massage on the organs of digestion. During deep inhalations and breath retention, the massage is stronger. This appears to work wonders. Constipation is banished. Kidney and urinary system problems disappear. The liver and the pancreas perform as never before. The digestive juices flow, and the stomach will assimilate anything.

Those who try, swear by it. Writes Swami Kuvalayananda:

> *From our own experience we can safely say that no physical exercise can even have one hundredth of the efficacy of Pranayama. In fact Pranayama is not only the control of the different physiological functions but it is the control of the very life processes that vitalize the human organism.*[1]

Yet, that is not all. Pranayama and Qi Gong calm the nerves; they allow a greater control than normal over the emotions and passions. They enhance vitality, mental clarity, and lovemaking. And they give a "natural high."

When a person's intake of oxygen increases, substances called endorphins are manufactured within the body. Endorphins exert a calming influence on the cerebral cortex; they appear to eliminate the effects of fear and terror and to induce a state of well-being. Endorphins are, incidentally, also produced by the administration of heroin. They are the human body's natural painkillers.

So much for the preventive aspect of health. Pranayama may avert disease, but Qi Gong purports to take things further. Its practice is known to have cured hypertension, cardiovascular diseases, gastroenteritis, asthma, neurasthenia, gynecological problems, and cancer.

According to Chinese theory, Qi defined is a material substance that enters the body in the form of oxygen. It is circulated through the two main channels in the trunk (the *Jin*) and the twelve minor channels (the *Lou*) leading to and from the limbs and organs. In time, due to poor eating and living habits, many of these channels become blocked. Qi no longer flows freely and stagnates in cavities, along the channels, called *Xue*. This results in disorders and diseases of the parts of the body affected by the blockage. The goal of Qi control is thus to clear the channels and cavities and to get the Qi flowing freely once again. Freely flowing Qi through the entire body means perfect health.

It is also an accepted fact, for many Chinese people, that when one has established control over one's Qi, it becomes possible to cure other people's ailments through the laying on of hands. I am not suggesting that you should take this at anything more than its curiosity value, yet, from the country of acupuncture and the miracles of *jiaoliang* (acu-flow), it might be worth investigating.

Chapter Three

—

The Preliminaries

Before getting to grips with Qi Gong and Pranayama exercises one must first consider the preliminaries: who can benefit from them, and where, when, and, of course, how they should be done.

Anyone and everyone can benefit from the practice of Oriental breathing exercises. There is no upper age limit either for practicing or for starting. Anyone who has seen a Chinese city in the early hours of the morning can vouch for that. The octogenarians exercising in the parks and squares in their hundreds are limbering up to their day with Qi Gong.

The younger one begins, the better. In Asia, children learn to do deep breathing as early as eight years old. They do not practice breath retention, however, until the body is more developed: at fourteen or fifteen.

Men and women benefit equally from breathing exercises. Women, in fact, derive the additional advantage that their internal organs of reproduction are given a salutary massage. Therapeutically this helps menstruation and childbirth since it ensures the correct position of the uterus. Breathing exercises should not, however, be practiced after the fourth month of pregnancy.

Normal health is an advantage for the beginner. Impaired health or convalescence are not the best conditions for beginning anything. Pranayama and Qi Gong are strenuous, even if only mildly so, therefore a condition of weakness may become more debilitating because of the effort. What, however, of those people who wish to practice Pranayama and Qi Gong specifically as a cure for illness? The same principle holds true: if one cannot be in the best of health, one should at least be as fit as possible considering the circumstances. To start experimenting with one's breathing in the middle of a fit of asthma is clearly rash. Somebody who has been practicing breathing exercises for some time may, on the other hand, continue through periods of illness or debilitation. With experience, overdoing it becomes less likely.

WHERE

The ancient texts are quite specific about the most suitable environment for practicing yoga and Pranayama. According to the *Gheranda Samhita*, one should practice Pranayama:

> *In a well-governed country, where one can get alms easily and where there is no nuisance, one should erect a hut having an enclosed compound. In the compound there should be a well or a pond. The cottage should be situated neither on too high nor on too low a site, and it should be free from insects. In the cottage so erected and smeared over with cow-dung, in such a secluded place one should practice Pranayama.*[1]

Swami Svatmarama's *Hathapradipika* offers similar advice:

> *A Hatha yogi should reside in solitude in a righteous country, where the government is benign and alms are easily available and which is free from all kinds of disturbances, in a small cottage having no rock, fire or water up to four cubits on any side.*[2]

This virtually debars anybody from even starting. Fortunately, not even the strictest spiritual culturist expects this sort of political utopia anymore. The rest of us need only privacy and fresh air. Ideally, one should practice Pranayama in one's own home. Somebody might run for the doctor if one were to go huffing and blowing anywhere else. A public gymnasium would be suitable for groups.

Pranayama is, however, a wholly individualistic form of exercise. A group situation may help initially in order to learn, or to ensure regularity of practice. Later, one should take one's own time at home.

The situation is different in the case of Qi Gong. Its Wai Dan exercises entail series of complex movements that would be difficult to learn and to practice on a person's own. Group practice should clearly be preferred wherever possible in order to ensure that sequences are remembered and performed correctly. The Chinese do this best when they fill the streets and parks in the early hours of the morning in their thousands.

Group practice is not the only reason the Chinese flood outdoors in all weather. The cramped living conditions in Chinese cities may have something to do with it. There is also the theory, however, that to practice Qi Gong most effectively one must be close enough to the earth to partake of its energy. One should therefore not practice above the fifth floor of a high-rise building. Outdoors, grass, or bare ground are better than cement pavement. Trees too are said to influence the efficacy of Qi Gong practice. "Good" trees to practice under are pines, redwoods, banyans, and weeping willows. "Bad" trees are said to be poplars, ginkgo bilobas, magnolias, and walnut and chestnut trees. Qi Gong masters hasten to point out that there exist no hard and fast rules as far as trees are concerned. Feelings about trees seems to be idiosyncratic. If you feel good doing Qi Gong under a poplar or a walnut, stick to it.

Wherever one chooses to practice, proper ventilation is indispensable. A closed, stuffy room is clearly not the best place to train one's lungs in, but a roaring draft is not too good either.

In the case of Pranayama, one can either sit or stand. A person may, if he or she wishes to, exercise the limbs with gentle movements (arm raising or walking, for example) but it is not generally advised as any movement tends to interfere with proper control of breathing. Pranayama therefore normally presupposes a seated posture (asana).

When one sits, one is instructed to do so cross-legged on a straw mat covered with a deer hide and a home-spun cotton blanket on top of that. Actually, any comfortable seat which allows one to sit with one's back straight and with hands on knees, is okay. The standing posture for Pranayama would be erect, legs slightly apart and hands on hips. Pranayama should not be performed lying down because, in this position, there is inadequate muscular activity for all the benefits to be felt.

Qi Gong is performed either sitting, standing, or with movement. Nei Dan Qi Gong is similar to Indian Pranayama and the same rules apply, except that in some exercises a lying down position is adopted. In "soft" Wai Dan Qi Gong (i.e., techniques that involve physical activity, but are not martial arts) the prescribed movements are slow and gentle and should not interfere with breathing. The practitioner must ensure that it is the Qi (breath) that governs the movement; not an undue exertion of the muscles which affects breathing.

WHEN

When to practice Pranayama or Qi Gong is really only a question of personal preference. A few suggestions might be useful nonetheless.

An ordinary Indian yogi bent on achieving liberation by means of Pranayama will probably dedicate between thirty and sixty minutes a day to the practice. Some may do more, but then it becomes an aberration, like those people who spend twenty years of their lives sitting in one place meditating, or those who clasp their fists until the nails grow through the flesh. Normally, then, the yogi does fifteen to thirty minutes of Pranayama twice a day, every day, morning and evening.

For purposes of physical culture, half that time is sufficient. Regularity is essential. One day off a week is admissible, but even that is best avoided. One day can easily become two, and two, three, until one finds oneself sitting down to a hurried stint of Pranayama once every two weeks, if that. It's better, therefore, to make a point of setting aside twenty minutes to practice breathing techniques every day, come what may.

The time of the day chosen for practice is immaterial. Most people prefer either before or after the rest of the day's activities. This generally means early morning or late evening, or sometime in the middle of the night. However, one should not be too tired. The main factor to consider, however, is the state of one's stomach. One should not be ravenous. Nor must Pranayama or Qi Gong ever be practiced close to a meal. If one were to do so, not only would no benefit result, but digestion might be impaired as a consequence. The most likely effect on the digestive system from the pressure pounding of pulmonary activity above it would be to vomit.

Four hours should thus elapse after a normal meal. And a person should not eat for half an hour after doing breathing exercises. When a light snack has been consumed, a two-hour wait is in order. After a cup of coffee or tea, half an hour should go by before getting down to the exercises.

Taking all this into consideration, one is, in effect, left with the morning, at least half an hour before breakfast, the evening, before dinner, and midnight.

In the morning one's joints are stiffer, which makes both sitting cross-legged and any exercise more difficult. On the other hand, early morning deep breathing is a worldwide remedy for lazy risers. Lastly, working overtime or social commitments may make regularity of practice more difficult in the evening. In the East, most physical culturists opt for the morning.

HOW

Washing

A shower before starting will give a person a feeling of freshness that will make breathing exercises more pleasurable. In India, a bath is considered of religious significance. It can mean anything from ritual ablutions in the Ganges to pouring a mug of water over one's head sitting in the gutter, but never a hot Western-style bathtub affair. Pranayama is also regarded as a religious practice. Pranayama and a bath therefore naturally go together. One can well do the same, although this is obviously not indispensable to successful practice. Just keep away from a hot bath; it is too debilitating.

Cleansing the nasal passages may also be useful. This practice is unheard of in the West. In India, however, nasal cleansing is as much a part of getting up as brushing the teeth and combing the hair. All the more reason, therefore, for the practitioner of breathing exercises to do it. Pranayama simply cannot be practiced unless the passage in both the nostrils is clear. Nasal cleansing is not generally done in China, but there is no reason why this useful exercise cannot be borrowed from India for Western practice of Chinese Qi Gong.

Nasal cleansing is of two types: cleaning the passage physically, and washing. The former is not as obnoxious as one might imagine. It is called Sutraneti: *neti* means "cleaning" and *sutra* means "a thread." Cleaning with a thread, twelve inches of soft cotton yarn, or a thin rubber catheter are the most common methods. Washing the inside of the nose is called Jalaneti, *jala* meaning "water."

Sutraneti: Take about a pint of water. Add a teaspoon of common salt. Put your sutra (catheter, yarn, or thick thread) in a saucepan together with the salted water. Bring to the boil so as to sterilize thoroughly. After allowing the water to cool (you can add cold tap water), remove the catheter and proceed to the bathroom. Do not throw the water away. You will need it later for your Jalaneti.

After washing your hands, stand over the wash basin, in front of the mirror. Now raise your head slightly so as to see your nostrils in the mirror. Take the catheter and push it slowly into the right nostril. Carry on pushing using the thumb and forefinger of each hand. There may be some discomfort at first when the tip of the catheter reaches about two inches into the nasal cavity. There is a bend here, so continue pushing ever so gently until your catheter is well into the nose and you feel a tickling sensation in your throat. The tip of the sutra must, in fact, emerge from the nasal cavity into the throat. Don't push too far or you will send it into your esophagus which is not pleasant. Now open your mouth and reach into it with either thumb and forefinger, or forefinger and middle finger, whichever you find easier. Get hold of the catheter and pull it gently out of your mouth. Holding each end of your sutra with thumbs and index fingers, you should now pull a couple of inches to and fro with each hand. This massages and cleanses the nasal passages thoroughly. After about a minute of this gentle massage, you should slowly pull the catheter out from your mouth.

The operation can now be repeated with the left nostril.

We are dealing with sensitive areas of mucous, so the point to bear in mind throughout this exercise is to be gentle and unhurried. If the catheter does not pass easily into the throat, do not insist. There may be a blockage caused by catarrh. In this case you should wash with Jalaneti and try again later.

Figure 1: Sutraneti

Jalaneti: Jalaneti follows Sutraneti in the same way that you rinse your mouth with water after brushing your teeth with toothpaste.

Transfer the lukewarm salted water, in which you had previously sterilized your sutra, from the saucepan to a small-sized teapot. Stand over the wash basin and insert the spout of the teapot into one of your nostrils. Tilt your head

Figure 2: Jalaneti

in the opposite direction from the teapot and slightly forward. Water should now be flowing from the teapot, into one nostril and out of the other one. Do not suck, blow, or breathe. Just let the water flow. When you think that teapot is half empty, straighten your head, remove the teapot spout, and blow the excess water out of your nose. Use the remainder of the water on the other nostril.

Clothing

Clothing should be loose and comfortable. That is all it amounts to. One should remove any clothing that constrains the top half of the body. In hot weather, being bare-chested is ideal. One should not, however, risk feeling cold, so a loose pajama top, shirt, or sweater may come in useful according to the weather.

Cotton clothes are preferable for both practical and esoteric reasons. Cotton is cool enough to offer protection without undue warmth—breathing exercises tend to increase body temperature. Cotton is also supposed to be permeable to Prana, or Qi, which means that, according to theory, it does not interfere with Qi circulation through the limbs as would, for example, synthetic material.

For the same reason, one should perform all exercises either barefoot or wearing only cotton socks. Any other footwear would isolate individual Qi, or Prana, from that of the earth. In any case it is more comfortable.

Exercise Routine

Pranayama and Qi Gong do not debar a person from practicing any other form of exercise or sport. In actual fact, breathing exercises lend themselves to being included in a vaster training program. Performance is enhanced and stamina improved. Perhaps the most well-known sportsman to make specific use of Pranayama in order to achieve outstanding results is the Frenchman Jaques Mayol, who for many years was the world-record holder for depth diving in apnea.

If Qi Gong and Pranayama are practiced in an exercise routine, they can either precede the more strenuous muscular activity, or follow after a twenty-minute rest. The point is that to practice Pranayama properly, the breathing must be controlled by the will, not by the body's demands for extra air.

Some exercises can be suitably combined with Pranayama. The most suitable are the postures of Hatha yoga. Wai Dan Qi Gong itself includes movement. Please refer, therefore, to the section on Wai Dan Qi Gong for a description of these techniques. Chapter 6 contains some suggested combinations of Hatha yoga and Pranayama exercises as practiced in India today.

Diet

Both Yoga and Qi Gong recommend light, nutritious vegetarian diets. It is claimed in Chinese tradition, that consuming the grosser Qi of animal flesh adversely affects one's own energy. In India, much emphasis is put on eating food that is "nutritious, sweet and unctuous, products of cow's milk and nourishing."[3]

Actually, what one eats is not either here nor there as far as the actual practice of Qi Gong and Pranayama are concerned. One should not, of course, overeat nor should one consume food which is clearly bad for the health.

Any precise definition of "good" or "bad" food for health is beyond the scope of a short manual of this sort, particularly in view of the vast and often contradictory research and literature that exists on healthy eating. However, certain general guidelines for achieving and maintaining health through good eating habits are recommended by both yoga and Qi Gong traditions.

One assertion that is generally made is that Qi Gong and Pranayama become futile by overeating. One is therefore supposed to eat sparingly—enough to fill three quarters of the stomach at each meal. A person should be able to rise from the dinner table feeling satisfied but never overindulged to the extent that digestion becomes difficult.

The actual foods recommended in India, are: whole grains, milk products, honey, dry ginger, vegetables, and fruit. What Svatmarama actually says is, eat "the good grains: wheat, rice, barley, milk, ghee [refined butter], sugar, butter, sugarcandy, honey, dry ginger, cucumber, the five leafy vegetables, green gram and rain-water collected during the tenth lunar month."[4]

One is warned against eating in excess: "Food which is bitter, sour, pungent, salty or hot, green vegetables, sour gruel, oil, mustard, and sesame," and from consuming "alcohol, fish, meat, curds, buttermilk, berries, oil-cakes, onion, and garlic." Nor should one eat "food that has been heated over again, dry, is excessively salty or sour, bad food, and food with excess of vegetables."[5]

Chinese Qi Gong masters offer similar advice. Food should be mild in taste, never heavy, hot, or spicy. Brown rice, whole meal corn, wheat, soybean products (including tofu), sweet potatoes, eggs, milk, cabbage, green leaf vegetables, carrots, honey, fruit, and *shitake* mushrooms are considered best for enhancing Qi.

Specific advice is given to people of extreme body build. It is said that very tall, thin people will achieve a better flow of Qi by eating plenty of fresh fruit, vegetables, soybean products, milk, eggs, and seafood. They should not eat meat or fish with scales nor strong yang foods, in other words, food that is spicy, hot, or salty.

Heavily built people who suffer from laziness and drowsiness would do well to consume plenty of fruit and vegetables, whole meal grains (brown rice and bread) and beans. They should refrain from eating dairy products, fats, and meat.

Meat is never recommended by Chinese masters except for people who lack yang (masculine) Qi. Basically this means people in an extremely weakened condition due to serious anemia, convalescence, or degenerative disease. In these circumstances, and only in these, Qi Gong teachers recommend fish, poultry, eggs, meat, and only small quantities of vegetables and fruit.

Both yoga and Qi Gong traditions state that food should be eaten raw whenever possible—most vitamins and enzymes are destroyed by heat. If cooking is necessary, food can be steamed, lightly boiled or sautéed, but never fried—fried oil is toxic. Sauces should be used sparingly if at all. Condiments and herbs may be added. Raw extra-virgin, unfiltered, and cold-pressed olive oil is considered by many health care practitioners to be the healthiest.

Fresh food is preferred whenever possible. The earlier food is consumed after purchase, the more wholesome it will be—some vitamins are dissipated in time. Frozen products are admissible only in extreme circumstances—vitamin C is destroyed by freezing. Canned food should never be eaten consisting as it does of pure bulk, with no enzymes or vitamins, plus megadoses of preservatives and other toxins. Sugars should be consumed in the form of fruit and honey, not refined or brown sugar or sweets.

Finally, raw food should be eaten at room temperature, and cooked food should be warm, never cold out of a refrigerator or piping hot—extremes in heat or cold are said to shock the system.

Drinks should be taken between meals; the ingestion of liquids while eating dilutes gastric juices thus making digestion more difficult. The healthiest drinks are water (distilled or mineral) at room temperature, warm, pure fruit juices, or herbal teas. Iced drinks, colas, alcohol, coffee, and tea are considered unhealthy.

Recommendations are made both in India and in China not only as to what to eat but also how to eat. One should sit down to one's meals unhurriedly and in a serene frame of mind. Being in a hurry, angry, and eating or emotionally upset interferes with the secretion of gastric juices and thus with proper digestion.

A person should chew food thoroughly. Digestion of starch begins with the action of saliva in the mouth. Thorough mastication therefore ensures better digestion. In China it is sometimes said that one should drink one's food and eat one's drinks.

A person should avoid being sedentary immediately after a meal. A popular Chinese saying claims that "one hundred steps after meals assures ninety-nine years of life."

Three meals a day are supposed to be most conducive to good health starting with a large breakfast followed by a medium-sized lunch and ending the day with a light dinner at least three hours before bedtime. Finally, yogic and Taoist traditions, but not that of modern-day Qi Gong, recommend an occasional fast in order to clear the body of toxins. Poor eating habits and overindulgence as well as pollutants and chemicals that make their way into the body through food require periodic cleansing. The safest and most effective method that has been practiced since antiquity is fasting.

Fasting

Fasts may be of two kinds: total or partial. A total fast is usually undergone by yogis twice a month—on the eleventh day after the full moon and on the eleventh day after no moon, hence the name for it, *Ekadasi*, or "eleventh day." The fast may last thirty-six hours, starting after the evening meal and ending with breakfast two days later. Others prefer a twenty-four-hour fast starting after either lunch or dinner and ending with lunch or dinner of the following day. No solid food at all should be consumed nor any drinks besides water. However, water must be drunk in large quantities in order to ensure that toxins are flushed out of the system.

Partial fasts usually last from three to ten days. They can be taken two to four times a year. No solid food is consumed, but organically grown apple, grape, strawberry, or watermelon pulp passed through a blender should be taken regularly. Other cleansing nutriments which should be ingested during a partial fast are spirulina, fibers such as bran, pure fruit juices, any fresh vegetable broth (including onion and garlic) without seasoning, and herbal teas. Only raw food should be eaten for two days before and two days after the fast has ended.

> **Caution:** Fasts lasting more than three days should be taken only with professional supervision. People suffering from diabetes and hypoglycemia should never fast without medical supervision.

Getting Down to It

The key factors in the actual practice of breathing exercises are regularity and moderation.

In order to feel the benefits of the exercises, a daily stint of twenty minutes should become as important in one's lifestyle as breakfast or morning coffee. When pressed for time, even ten minutes is better than nothing at all.

The benefits will, however, be felt slowly. As the Chinese say, "It takes a hundred days to achieve one step, a thousand days to achieve many." It is no use rushing headlong into Pranayama and Qi Gong and expect miracles to happen overnight. One must start gently, and work gradually up to the more difficult exercises. As with all new exercises, too much too fast can be counterproductive if not downright dangerous.

Some general hints may be in order now concerning the mode of inspiration and expiration in Pranayama and Nei Dan Qi Gong. We shall, of course, go into greater detail on this when describing the various exercises. As a general rule, inhalation should last about half the time taken to exhale. Both inhalation and expiration must be uniform. In other words, there should be no changes in the flow of air either at the beginning, middle, or end of the act. Every inspiration must end gently. When the lungs are comfortably full, there can be no advantage in contracting the muscles, vainly trying to force a little more air in. The same is true for exhalation. One must begin and end each breath gently.

Having said that, we leave you to the exercises themselves.

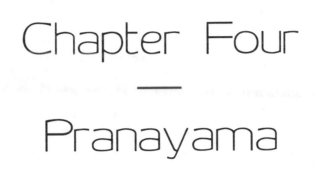

Chapter Four

—

Pranayama

Although no hard and fast rules exist as to where, when, and how Pranayama must be practiced, certain guidelines will be necessary for the beginner. Once the general principles have been understood, one may experiment and find one's own rhythm, favorite position, place, and form of exercise. Therefore, this book looks at what traditional yogic texts have to say on the subjects of seating, posture, hand positions, locks—or bandhas—and fundamental breathing techniques.

Try each position and technique and turn and settle to down to the one with which you feel most comfortable.

THE SEAT

The traditional seat is a straw mat covered with a deer hide and a cotton cloth. A thick carpet, a folded blanket, or a hard cushion will do. The point is to assure yourself a firm and comfortable base to sit on. You should not feel discomfort from a hard and cold floor, neither should the steadiness of your back posture be impaired by a seat which is too soft.

THE POSTURE

Five postures are advised by the classic texts. In inverse order of difficulty, these are: Padmasana, or the Lotus pose; Siddhasana, the posture of the successful yogi; Swastikasana, which means with legs crossed; Vajrasana, or the phallic pose, and Sukhasana, the easy posture. All of these positions might entail some degree of discomfort to someone with sore knee joints. If the traditional positions do prove uncomfortable, there is absolutely no reason why Pranayama cannot be performed sitting on a chair. It is important, however, not to lounge, but to sit erect with hands on thighs or placed palms upward, one over the other on your lap.

Padmasana

The Lotus pose is the traditional position for meditation. It is called Lotus because the position of the feet and of the hands is supposed to imitate the figure of a lotus flower in bloom. In addition, many statues of the Buddha show him seated in this position on top of a flowering lotus.

To achieve the position you should sit with your legs stretched in front of you. Bend your right knee and with the help of both your hands, place your right foot on your left thigh with the sole turned upward. Now place your left foot on your right thigh so that your heels nearly touch. Both your knees should be firmly on the ground. Hold your back and your head straight. Place your hands, palms upward, on your heels with your left hand underneath your right. The position of the hands with thumbs and fingers overlapping one another, is said to resemble an open lotus flower. During alternate nostril breathing in Pranayama, the right hand will be used to close the nostril while the left hand will remain in place on your heels.

The general sensation while seated in Padmasana should be one of stability, although, if you have never done it before, there will probably be some pain in your hip joints and perhaps in your ankles. If the pain is too strong or if you find the position impossible, not to worry; Pranayama can be performed perfectly well without sitting in the Lotus pose. However, if you feel only mildly uncomfortable and would like to adopt this posture with greater ease, there are three exercises which can help.

Figure 3: Padmasana

Loosening the ankles: Sit with both legs stretched out in front of you. Bend your right leg and hold the ankle firmly in your right hand. Place hand and knee on your left thigh just above your left knee. Hold the foot with your left hand and guide the foot in a wide circular motion while holding the ankle in place against your thigh with your right hand. Repeat the exercise with

Figure 4: Loosening the ankles

your left foot. Care must be taken not to exert too much pressure on the ankle.

Loosening the hip joints: Sit on the ground with both legs bent at the knees. Hold the soles of the feet against one another with both hands. Pull your feet as close to your body as possible while keeping them on the ground. Holding your feet firmly toward your body, alternatively lower and raise your knees in a fairly rapid flapping motion. Do not force, and do not exert any pressure on your knees.

Figure 5: Loosening the hip joints

Loosening the ankles, hips, and knees: Sit on the ground with your legs straight. Bend your right knee and hold the ankle with your left hand against your left knee. Lean slightly forward and, with your right hand, press your right knee against the floor. Always lower the knee gently. If you cannot touch the floor with it, press it down as far as it will comfortably go but do not use force. Stop exercising if you feel any pain in your knee.

Figure 6: Loosening the ankles, hips, and knees

Five or six minutes' practice of these exercises should enable you to achieve the Lotus pose with ease within two or three months at the most.

> **Caution:** Never exert yourself beyond what is only mildly uncomfortable. Forcing your legs into positions you are not used to can cause lasting damage to the joints, muscles, and ligaments.

Siddhasana

Siddhi means "mystic power," and a siddha is a person who has, through the practice of yoga, achieved this power. Siddhasana is considered, by yogis, to be the most favorable position for obtaining siddhis.

To achieve this position, place your left heel against your perineum. This is the area between the genitals and the anus. Bring your right foot across and place the toes in the crevice between the calf and the thigh of your left leg. The heel of your right foot must press against the pubic bone. Your hands should rest on your knees.

In Siddhasana, the legs and the lower back are stretched to a greater extent than in other yogic seated postures. The heels are on the same perpendicular as the genitals, and the pressure exerted by them, one below and the other above the

genitals, is supposed to arouse the serpent power of the Kundalini. Most people will, however, find this position to be one of the least comfortable to maintain for more than a few minutes. Sitting on a thick book helps, but many might prefer to tackle the Swastikasana instead.

Figure 7: Siddhasana

Caution: It is claimed by some commentators that Siddhasana maintained for long periods can lead to temporary impotence in men.

Swastikasana

In the Swastikasana the shins cross one another and the toes are placed against the inner hollow of the knees imitating the shape of the swastika cross.

You should sit cross-legged with your left heel against your right groin. Your right foot should by placed on your left thigh. Your legs will cross just above your ankles. As in Siddhasana, your

Figure 8: Swastikasana

hands should rest on your knees. Your back and neck must be held straight.

Vajrasana

Anyone who finds cross-legged positions difficult may feel more comfortable in the Vajrasana kneeling posture. *Vajra*, in Sanskrit, means "phallus." The asana is so called because the knees and thighs in this position are supposed to look like giant penises, though it takes a peculiar mind to see it.

In Vajrasana you should kneel with knees together and then sit on your ankles. To be more precise, your toes should be touching and your heels apart so that you are sitting between your heels, not on them. Your back should be erect, and your hands placed on your thighs.

Figure 9 A, B & C: Vajrasana

Sukhasana

Sukhasana means "pleasurable posture" and is described in the *Upanishads* as follows:

"In whatever sitting position one may attain comfort and steadiness, that is called Sukhasana. It is to be assumed by the weak."

In practice, Sukhasana means sitting with your legs crossed and your back straight. You should rest the palms of your hands on your knees. The closer your knees are to the ground the better. If your knees refuse to lower and you find yourself toppling over backward, you might try sitting on a thick book. With time, you will find the position more comfortable, and the book can then be dispensed with.

Figure 10: Sukhasana

Shavasana

Pranayama should only be practiced in Shavasana when a person is feeling particularly weak and tired, or while convalescing after an illness. *Shava* means "corpse." In fact, the position resembles

Figure 11: Shavasana

that of a stretched out corpse. Just lie on your back with your feet six inches apart and your arms along the side of your body.

Shavasana is a relaxing pose that is normally adopted in between Hatha yoga exercises. Only the gentlest forms of Pranayama can be practiced in it.

Mudra, the Position of the Hands

We have mentioned that in most Pranayama postures, the hands rest on the knees, thighs, or lap. The actual hand positions are not of prime importance; it is sufficient that they feel relaxed. However, yogic tradition does recommend a specific position of the hands, or Mudra, when they are rested on the knees.

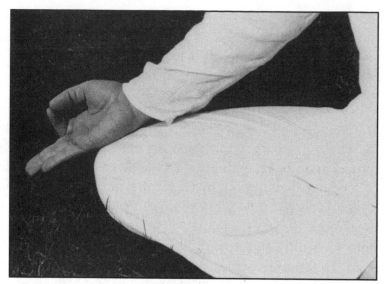

Figure 12: Jnana-Mudra

This is called Jnana-Mudra, or the "symbol of knowledge." It is commonly used during *dhyana,* or meditation.

In Jnana-Mudra the hands are placed palms upward on the knees. Three fingers are held straight while the index finger is bent to form a circle with the thumb. In theory this is supposed to help the flow of Prana through the body.

BREATHING THROUGH THE NOSTRILS

During the practice of Pranayama all inhalations and exhalations will take place through your nostrils, except where otherwise specified. It is only when breathing through the nose that a person can, in fact, achieve proper control over respiration.

Sometimes you will be using both your nostrils together. Sometimes, you will be inhaling through one nostril and exhaling out of the other, alternating after each breath. For more information about alternate nostril breathing, see page 51.

The Essentials: Puraka, Rechaka, and Kumbhaka

Puraka means "inhalation," rechaka means "exhalation," and kumbhaka means "retention." They are the three essential components of Pranayama.

Puraka is a slow, deep, and uniform inhalation through the nostrils. Starting from the lower chest, the lungs must be filled slowly and completely. Although all the lungs will be fully expanded, the abdominal wall should not bulge. There should be no variation in the rate at which air is drawn in, either at the beginning, middle, or at the end of each puraka. Every puraka must end quietly. No amount of effort or violent muscular contraction at the end of an inhalation can help to draw in more air. All purakas performed in a given sitting of Pranayama should be of uniform duration.

Rechaka is a controlled, uniform, and complete exhalation through the nose. As in the case of puraka, each rechaka must begin and end quietly, without effort. The proper ratio between puraka and rechaka is 1:2. A typical five-second inhalation should thus be followed by an exhalation lasting ten seconds. If you find it easier to spend the same time on both inhalation and exhalation, there is no harm in doing this. Normally, however, the muscular activity involved in puraka calls for less time than the more passive act of allowing the lungs to deflate during rechaka.

To begin with, it is advisable to practice Pranayama by concentrating on the depth and regularity of puraka and rechaka. As an aid to maintaining a uniform flow of breath during both inhalation and expiration it can be useful to contract the throat slightly. By partially closing the glottis (the elongated fissure in the throat between the vocal cords), a humming sound is produced with each puraka and rechaka. A low pitched and uniform hum is proof of a correct breathing technique. After two or three months of regular practice, when you have mastered the fundamentals of inhalation and exhalation, you may, if you wish, move on to the third component of Pranayama called kumbhaka, or breath retention.

Kumbhaka consists of holding the breath for five to thirty seconds after each inhalation. The purpose of kumbhaka is to exert additional pressure within the body, thus enhancing the internal massaging effect of deep breathing.

Kumbhaka must be performed naturally and without effort. When it is first practiced, it should last no longer than the time taken for the breath to be inhaled: around five seconds. Later, this time can be extended gradually up to twenty seconds or, in cases of exceptional athletic prowess, to thirty seconds.

> **Caution:** Kumbhaka is dangerous and if misused can cause permanent damage to your heart and lungs. Great care must therefore be taken never to exceed your natural capacity for holding your breath during the practice of Pranayama. A sure sign that you are overdoing it is when, at the end of the kumbhaka, you are unable to exhale slowly and uniformly. If the subsequent inhalation is also forced and hurried, it is time to break off and breathe normally for a few minutes before continuing.

Kumbhaka should thus always be performed, without effort, as a comfortable retention of your breath after each puraka in a given sitting. Starting with five-second kumbhakas, you can, after being confidently established in that pattern, extend the time to ten seconds, then fifteen and, finally, twenty. It normally takes a student of Pranayama six months of steady practice to reach this level of proficiency. The point is, and it cannot be overemphasized, that you must never exceed your own limits.

The practice of kumbhaka is nearly always accompanied by a bandha, or lock.

Bandhas

Bandha, in Sanskrit, means "binding or knot." A bandha is the contraction of particular muscles in order to lock the air, or Prana, in the body. The classic texts on yoga mention four bandhas: Jalandhara Bandha, Uddiyana Bandha, Mula Bandha, and Jivha Bandha. Only the first three are practiced with any frequency.

Jalandhara Bandha: the most common bandha. It is normally used in conjunction with kumbhaka breath retention. Jala means net or network and refers to the network of channels (called nadis) in the throat. This bandha is practiced by holding the breath, bending the neck forward and pressing the chin against the base of the collar bone. Svatmarama's *Hathapradipika* describes it:

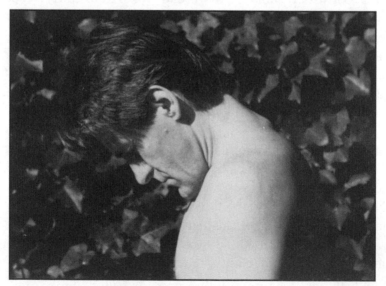

Figure 13: Jalandhara Bandha

Contracting the throat, the chin should be firmly placed on the chest. This is known as Jalandhara Bandha. It prevents old age and a premature death.[1]

Although a person may legitimately question the life-extending properties of Jalandhara Bandha, its usefulness during the practice of kumbhaka is worth pointing out.

First of all, kumbhaka is easier with the neck bent than when it is held straight. The sharp bend in the neck holds the breath in without putting undue pressure on the muscles around the glottis. Furthermore, when pent up air is released at the end of the kumbhaka, it may force open the Eustachian, or auditory, tubes, and cause damage to the internal ear. The Jalandhara chin lock prevents this onrush of air and thus provides a valuable defense against the danger of ear damage.

Uddiyana Bandha means "raising up lock." During this bandha, the thoracic diaphragm is pulled upward under an expanded rib cage. While Jalandhara Bandha is an aid to proper breath retention during the practice of Pranayama, Uddiyana Bandha is really an exercise in its own right. It stretches and massages the internal organs of the abdomen, improves circulation to these organs, and removes congestion.

Uddiyana Bandha can be performed either sitting or standing. When sitting in one of the cross-legged Pranayama positions, lean slightly forward and place your hands on your knees. Your fingers should be on the inside of your knees (see figure 14). When standing, keep your feet about eighteen inches apart and bend your knees slightly. Lean forward and place your hands on your thighs just above your knees. Your fingers must, again, be on the inside of your thighs. Arching your back a little, support the full weight of your upper body on your hands.

When the position has been achieved, exhale as much air as you possibly can from your lungs. Now, holding your breath, take a vigorous mock inhalation. Your rib cage will expand and your diaphragm will be pulled upward by the internal vacuum. For Uddiyana to be performed successfully, the muscles of the abdomen must be completely relaxed. The expansion of the rib cage during the mock inhalation will thus draw in the walls of the abdomen giving a pronounced concave appearance (see figure 15). Hold the position for as long as is comfortable. When you can no longer hold your breath, relax your neck and shoulders and inhale slowly allowing the abdomen to return gradually to its normal position.

Three or four rounds of Uddiyana a day are sufficient for its benefits to be felt.

The Benefits: It massages the internal organs of the abdomen and can eliminate constipation, indigestion, dyspepsia, intestinal gasses, and liver problems.

Caution: Not for people suffering from circulatory or cardiovascular problems. To be performed with care when serious abdominal disorders exist.

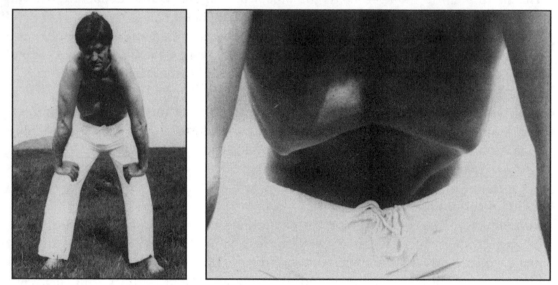

Figures 14 & 15: Uddiyana Bandha

Mula Bandha: Mula means "root or base." This bandha is performed primarily on the anal sphincters. As with Uddiyana, Mula Bandha is an exercise in its own right; it is normally performed in conjunction with Uddiyana.

On its own, Mula Bandha can be practiced in Siddhasana. In this posture, pressure is exerted on the perineum by the heel, thus purportedly arousing the coiled serpent of the Kundalini. This, however, may not necessarily be your intention, in which case, Siddhasana can be dispensed with. Mula Bandha can be done in any other seated position of your choice.

The exercise consists of forcibly contracting the anal sphincters during the retention of breath. The contraction of the sphincters necessarily exercises the whole of the pelvic region. Hence, Mula Bandha is really an exercise in pelvic contraction.

When performed during the mock inhalation stage of Uddiyana, Mula Bandha enhances the effects of both exercises.

> **The Benefits:** It is said to arouse the Kundalini, which is another way of explaining that it acts on the central and sympathetic nervous systems through the nerve terminals in the anal sphincters. It helps the bodily functions of digestion, circulation, endocrine hormone secretion, and defecation.

> **Caution:** Mula Bandha incorrectly performed can lead to constipation and digestive upsets. Incorrect practice has also been known to cause soreness to the genitals and consequent minor and temporary impotence.

Jivha Bandha: Jivha, in Sanskrit, means "tongue." This bandha is essentially only a variety of Jalandhara wherein the tongue is pressed against the roof of the mouth. Its usefulness is in exercising the root of the tongue and its adjoining tissues.

> **The Benefits:** When practiced with the Jalandhara chin lock, Jivha Bandha provides additional defense against a sudden onrush of pent-up air from the lungs, which might cause damage to the inner ears. It also exercises the root of the tongue and its adjoining tissues.

> **Caution:** None.

MAKING A START

Take a seat, close your eyes, and breathe normally through your nose. It pays, before doing anything else, to watch yourself breathing quietly.

You will notice, with the help of watch with a visible seconds hand—and with your eyes open —that it takes four to five seconds to breathe in and out: this means that you make about a dozen respirations a minute. You will also notice that your ordinary breathing is shallow and comes nowhere near to utilizing the full capacity of your lungs.

Watching yourself breathing has probably affected the rate and depth of your inhalations already, so now take control of your respiration and consciously expand your lungs as far as is comfortable for each successive breath. Breathe in and out deeply and without pausing. Do this for ten breaths and note down the time you have taken.

On your second sitting, try deep, continuous breathing again. Your aim is to achieve a steady uniformity for each successive breath. It doesn't matter how long it takes you to complete ten rounds of respiration—it can be anything between two and five minutes—the point is that the time taken must be the same for each sitting. When you feel that you have achieved this—normally after three days to a week— you can gradually increase the number of breaths at each sitting from ten to twenty. Continue to time yourself during each session.

You may, at this stage, introduce a new technique that will ensure that each breath is performed uniformly.

By contracting your throat and half closing the glottis, you will hear a low hum with each inhalation and expiration. Any variation in this sound means lack of steadiness in your breathing. When, therefore, you are able to produce a uniform hum with each breath, you can be confident that you have achieved proficiency in the first stage of simple puraka-rechaka Pranayama.

Your next concern will be to pay attention to the time ratio between your purakas and rechakas. This should be 1:2. When you are able to breathe out steadily and comfortably in twice the time it takes you to breathe in, for an entire sitting of twenty rounds, you are on the verge of real breath control.

You are now ready to increase the length of each round. Steadily, over the next twenty to thirty sessions, you should strive to prolong each puraka and rechaka. Your goal should be to achieve a ten-second puraka followed by a twenty-second rechaka, for a minimum of twenty successive rounds. If this proves difficult, or causes discomfort, slow down, or settle for a twenty-second round instead. It is important never to exceed your physical limits.

Once you feel that you are comfortable with extended deep breathing, you may, if you wish, introduce kumbhaka breath retention into your practice, or experiment with other, more advanced methods of Pranayama or Qi Gong. However, for ordinary fitness and health purposes, a daily session of twenty rounds of puraka and rechaka is adequate. Remember that the benefits of Pranayama are felt with time. The more regularly you practice, the greater the advantage.

INCORRECT PRACTICE OF PRANAYAMA

When Pranayama is performed properly, it confers definite benefits in terms of health and fitness. Errors of practice, on the other hand, may give rise to discomfort and even to disorders of quite a serious nature. It is therefore of primary importance to recognize the effects of incorrect Pranayama practice.

Pranayama is performed correctly when no excesses are committed, when one does not rush ahead, putting undue strain on oneself in order to achieve quick results, and when one emerges from one's daily stint feeling relaxed, satisfied, and refreshed.

The first sign of incorrect practice is the inability to inhale or exhale slowly and steadily. If this happens, it means that you are probably holding your breath too long, or making an unnatural effort to breathe out. Feelings of suffocation usually derive from the same mistakes. The remedy, in both cases, is to breathe normally for a few minutes before continuing with Pranayama.

Should you feel tired or bored at the end of a sitting, it probably means that you are overdoing it, or have been practicing distractedly with other concerns on your mind. In this case, it is a good idea to shorten your sitting for the next day or two. At the end of a good session, you should always feel that you still have the energy and the will to do a few more rounds.

Heaviness, stomachache, and mild diarrhea can occur after practicing Pranayama. The usual cause is exercising too close to a meal. At least three hours, and possibly four, should elapse after a meal before getting down to Pranayama.

Other unusual effects may occur during, or after, the practice of Pranayama. Not all of these are indicative of incorrect techniques, however. Many of them are temporary and will disappear when your body has grown accustomed to the increased circulation of Prana.

Dizziness: The increased flow of oxygen to the brain can give rise to fits of dizziness. This occurs quite frequently during prolonged Kapalabhati (see chapter 5). The remedy is to slow down or stop exercising.

Soreness in the joints, the abdomen, or the thighs: Exercising parts of the body that are seldom subjected to any unusual movements or positions leads inevitably to some soreness. It will pass in a few days. Should the pains persist, the cause may be found elsewhere: an uncomfortable seat, undue exertion, or incorrect technique. If you continue to be unable to find the cause, consult a doctor.

Intestinal and stomach gas: Pranayama stimulates all the organs of digestion. Stomach and intestinal rumblings, belching, and passing gas are common reactions in the early stages of practice. They are nothing to worry about; even if they cause some embarrassment, these effects are temporary.

Rapid heartbeat and fluttering pulse: These are natural reactions that can accompany the early stages of Pranayama practice. Unless they continue after several weeks of practice or occur when not exercising, there is nothing to be concerned about. A too rapid heartbeat after several weeks of Pranayama practice probably means that you are over exerting yourself. Slow down.

Numbness in the legs: Your seat is either too hard or you have been sitting in one of the cross-legged postures too long. Go for a stroll or change your position.

Itching or prickly sensations of the skin, sensations of heat or cold in the limbs: These reactions are incidental to the increased intake of oxygen into the body. Ignore them, steady your mind, and concentrate on something concrete: the color of the wallpaper, the dust on the carpet, or the shape of your toenail. Again, these feelings are transitory.

Irrational sensations in the limbs and in the head, visual and auditory hallucinations, sudden emotion: These rarely occur, but if they do, recognize them as the effects of increased oxygen intake. Ignore them and, as above, concentrate on something else. The possibilities are infinite.

Increased appetite: This is one of the healthy aspects of Pranayama practice. It may not be just for food, either. Pranayama and Qi Gong teachers believe, however, that an increased urge for sex should not be indulged in overenthusiastically. This would only be debilitating. The new Prana, or Qi, energy circulating in the body should not, they argue, be discharged before it has had time to strengthen the body as a whole.

....

....

....

Chapter Five

—

Pranayama Techniques

Once you feel you are comfortable with extended deep breathing, have mastered the basics of puraka, rechaka, and kumbhaka, and have settled down to a daily exercise program, you will probably want to expand your horizons further and experiment with the advanced methods of Pranayama and Qi Gong.

Try each of the techniques at least once, learn what they entail, and then include your favorites in your daily exercise routine. Practice regularly and stick to the same techniques. Remember that it is only by digging one deep well will you find water, not by jumping around from place to place.

ALTERNATE NOSTRIL BREATHING

A technique that can usefully be included in the early stages of Pranayama is breathing through alternate nostrils.

First of all it helps the beginner to achieve greater control over his or her respiration. When only one nostril is used for inhalation, the degree of steadiness of the incoming flow can be more easily perceived and regulated. The same is true for rechaka.

Second, controlled alternate nostril breathing exerts a balancing effect on the vagaries of one nostril's predominance over the other. In normal breathing, the air seldom flows equally through both nostrils. Sometimes it is the left nostril that is dominant, sometimes the right. For most people, this seems to alternate about once every two hours.

In Tantric and Hatha Yogic theory, the right nostril is identified with masculine and solar breath (*Ha*), and the left nostril is feminine and lunar (*Tha*). The equilibrium of the two breaths (Hatha) is the ideal toward which the yogi should be striving. Tantric texts claim that by balancing the masculine and the feminine breaths, the yogi achieves *moksha*, or liberation.

Dr. Pratap, from the Kaivalyadhama Institute of Yoga in Lonavla, India, takes a more scientific view of the benefits of balancing the air flow through the two nostrils. He writes:

> *It is possible that central mechanisms govern nostril breathing in order to maintain homeostasis of the organism. Therefore sometimes right nostril breathing is dominant, and sometimes left nostril breathing. Sometimes breathing takes place equally through both nostrils. It may be surmised that the air currents passing through the right nostril influence excitatory effects, while those passing through the other nostril produce inhibitory effects. As per the claim of this science of breath, it could be used in family planning, diagnosis, prognosis of diseases and the cure.*[1]

The technique of alternate breathing is extremely simple. It consists of using the thumb of your right hand to block your right nostril while you inhale through the other. When the puraka is complete, block your left nostril with the third finger of the same hand, and breathe out through your right nostril. At the end of the rechaka, breathe in again through the same nostril, and breathe out through the other. Change nostril only after inhaling, never after an exhalation.

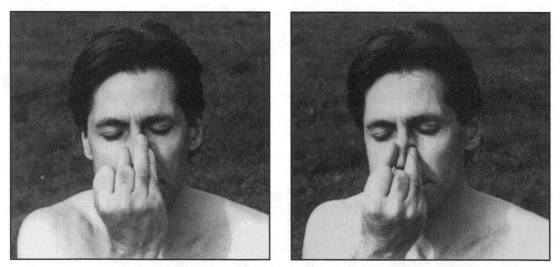

Figure 16 A & B: Vishnu Mudra, position of hand

Yoga texts recommend the following technique for closing your nostrils. Bend your index and middle fingers against your palm. Your thumb and two other fingers should be kept straight. Close your right nostril by pressing your thumb against the side of your nose so that the whole passage is occluded. The other fingers should rest gently on the bridge of your nose. To close your left nostril press the left side of your nose against the septum with your third finger. Rest your thumb on the bridge of your nose. Tradition recommends the use of your right hand. Your left hand should rest on your lap. Left-handed people may, however, find it easier to invert this position.

Outer Kumbhaka, Holding the Breath Out

Traditional Pranayama envisages only one way of performing kumbhaka, holding breath out. It is by holding the breath in at the end of the puraka. For specific therapeutic purposes, however, it may be useful to hold the breath at the end of the rechaka.

An outer kumbhaka should be preceded by adequate ventilation of the lungs; thirty seconds of Kapalabhati (see below) would be ideal. On the last stroke, expel as much air as you can, adopt the Jalandhara Bandha, and hold your breath for as long as is comfortable. Release the lock and breathe normally for a minute or two before repeating the exercise. Four or five rounds of outer kumbhaka are enough to begin with. These may be gradually extended to ten, within a month.

To follow your rounds of outer kumbhaka with a few minutes of ordinary Pranayama including inward breath retention, enhances the therapeutic value of both.

> **Caution:** You should not combine inner and outer kumbhaka in the same round. The strain on your respiratory system would simply neutralize any positive effects that the exercise might otherwise have.

Kapalabhati, the Cleansing Breath

Strictly speaking, Kapalabhati is not part of Pranayama, but is essentially a purification practice. Kapalabhati, or shining skull exercise (*kapala*, in Sanskrit, means "skull," and *bhati* "shining"), is designed to cleanse the sinuses and the nerve channels until the skull shines—figuratively speaking, of course. In actual fact, Kapalabhati ensures an increased intake of oxygen, and the rapid elimination of carbon dioxide and water vapor from the lungs. Because of this, Kapalabhati should be performed before starting your ordinary Pranayama routine. More oxygen and less carbon dioxide in your blood guarantee greater ease in controlling slow breathing. They also allow longer breath retention times. If you are practicing kumbhaka, you will be able to prolong your retention times quite easily if you break your Pranayama into three successive sessions with short bouts of Kapalabhati in between.

The ideal posture for the practice of Kapalabhati is the Lotus pose, or Padmasana. The vigorous abdominal contractions that this exercise calls for are liable to impair the stability of any less secure posture. Your hands may be placed on your lap or on your knees.

During Kapalabhati, puraka and rechaka take place through the nose, as usual. However, this exercise differs from Pranayama in that attention is paid exclusively to rechaka, while puraka is ignored. Rechaka in Kapalabhati is accomplished by means of short vigorous contractions of the front abdominal muscles. Puraka then becomes a passive act that takes place when the abdominal muscles are relaxed.

Begin by taking a deep breath through both nostrils, then pull in the abdomen sharply and raise your diaphragm so as to force the air suddenly out of your nose. It will sound rather like a sneeze. Immediately the exhalation is finished, relax your abdominal muscles, and your next inhalation will take place automatically. Force the air out again in the same manner. Repeat the exercise a dozen times at a rate of one exhalation a second.

After a minute's rest you may do another dozen rounds of Kapalabhati, and again, after another minute of ordinary breathing.

With a few days of practice, you can increase the rate of your rechakas to two per second. Faster than that would impair the efficacy of the exercise. You may also increase the length of each sitting to the maximum number of rapid exhalations that you can do before tiring and losing your rhythm. This generally means thirty seconds at the most.

Most people are able to do Kapalabhati correctly the first time they try. Some beginners may, however, forget to relax their abdominal muscles after each rechaka, thus preventing the automatic inflow of air during puraka. Take care, therefore, not to make any effort to inhale the air. Concentrate on rechaka only.

> **The Benefits:** In normal breathing, a person inhales about 500 millileters of air with each breath, about seven liters, or 14.8 pints, of air a minute. During Kapalabhati this is increased to 600 millileters per breath which, at a rate of 120 breaths per minute, means seventy liters, or 150 pints, of air each minute. A tenfold increase, therefore. More air means an enriched bloodstream, better oxidization of all the cells of the body, and

a faster elimination of carbon dioxide waste. The rapid breathing also has a marked warming effect on the body to the extent that it is said that some yogis use Kapalabhati to keep warm when sitting naked in the snow in the higher reaches of the Himalayas.

Kapalabhati clears the nasal passages and the nerve channels. It improves circulation and digestion. The latter is helped by the obvious massaging effect that the exercise has on the abdominal viscera.

Finally, Kapalabhati prepares the body for Pranayama by establishing an enriched metabolic condition that decreases subsequent oxygen requirements. Respiration thus slows down automatically, and assures the practitioner greater control over the slow breathing techniques essential to Pranayama.

Caution: Kapalabhati is too vigorous for anyone suffering from pulmonary or heart problems. It is not to be attempted, therefore, by anyone who has these problems, without first seeking medical advice.

Everyone of average health can only benefit from Kapalabhati although the huge increase in the intake of oxygen may give rise to feelings of dizziness or, on occasion, to the mild visual and auditory hallucinations mentioned in chapter 4.

A slight soreness of the abdominal muscles is likely to follow your first attempts at Kapalabhati. This will disappear as soon as the muscles tone up.

Bhastrika, the Bellows Breath

Bhastrika is sufficiently similar to Kapalabhati to be often confused with it. Indeed, Bhastrika differs from Kapalabhati only to the extent that kumbhaka (breath retention) is introduced at the end of each round. Technically speaking, the introduction of kumbhaka makes Bhastrika one of the varieties of traditional Pranayama. It is recognized as such by Svatmarama. He describes Bhastrika as follows:

Being well-settled in Padmasana, the wise should, with neck and body held erect, close the mouth and forcefully exhale through the nostrils, making a sound so that exhalation is felt in the chest, throat and top of the skull; then he should breathe in quickly till the inhaled air reaches the region of the heart.

He should exhale and inhale in the same manner again and again. Air should be carefully moved in and out of one's body in the manner in which the blacksmith works his bellows rapidly.

This can only be done by the action of the abdominal wall. When physical fatigue sets in, the yogi should inhale through the right nostril. He should completely fill the thoracic cavity with air quickly; then hold the nose tightly without using his middle and index finger and, performing kumbhaka as prescribed, should throw the air out through the left nostril. [2]

It is clear from this description that Bhastrika is accomplished by means of the same bellows-like abdominal technique as Kapalabhati. Hence the name. *Bhastrika* in Sanskrit means "bellows."

Take your seat and go through a round of rapid abdominal breathing as described for Kapalabhati. At the end of this round (not more than twenty exhalations are recommended by some texts[3]), breathe in as deeply as possible, remembering, however, to do so slowly and uniformly. You should try to make this puraka last at least eight seconds.

Retain the air by closing your nostrils as advised by Svatmarama, and drop your head forward until your chin presses against your neck in the Jalandhara Bandha. Hold your breath for as long as is comfortable.

When you are ready to do so, let go of your nose, lift your head, and exhale slowly so that your rechaka lasts twice as long as your previous inhalation.

You have now completed one round of Bhastrika. Breathe normally for a minute or two, and you are ready to continue. The *Gheranda Samhita* recommends three rounds of Bhastrika in one sitting, and most experts would agree:

A wise man should perform this Bhastrika three times. There will be no disease or suffering. Day by day he will gain in health.[4]

We have described the most straightforward variety of Bhastrika. You will notice, however, that Svatmarama's *Hathapradipika* recommends alternate nostril breathing during the second, deep breathing stage of Bhastrika. There are, in fact, three variations of this Pranayama exercise. They are as follows:

First variation: The one described in *Hathapradipika*. After the rapid abdominal breathing stage, the deep puraka and rechaka are performed through alternate nostrils. Breathe in slowly through the right nostril. Retain the breath in Jalandhara Bandha. Exhale through your left nostril.

Second variation: The glottis is kept partially closed during the rapid breathing stage of Bhastrika. The final slow puraka and rechaka may be performed either with both nostrils or by alternating them.

Third variation: Alternate nostril breathing is used during the "bellows" part of Bhastrika. The rapid coordination required between the fingers closing the alternate nostrils and the quick abdominal expirations may take some time to master. Use your right hand as described in alternate nostril breathing. Inhale through your right nostril and exhale through your left. Inhale through your left and exhale through your right. Alternate in this manner, changing nostril after each inhalation by releasing one nostril at the same time as you close the other.

The second slow deep breathing stage is again performed through alternate nostrils. Breathe in through the right, retain, and exhale through the left.

> **The Benefits:** Svatmarama's *Hathapradipika* claims that Bhastrika "...cures the diseases of wind, bile and phlegm and increases the gastric fire."[5] Actually, Bhastrika gives the same benefits as Kapalabhati with the additional advantage derived from the final deep puraka, kumbhaka, and rechaka. Therefore, Bhastrika:
>
> - Increases oxygen input, thus purifying the bloodstream
> - Cleanses the nasal passages and the nerve channels
> - Improves circulation and digestion
> - Massages the abdominal viscera
> - Warms the body
> - Tones up the nervous system and the muscles of respiration
> - Prevents degenerative diseases
>
> **Caution:** Bhastrika is a vigorous respiratory exercise that can be harmful to anyone suffering from heart or pulmonary troubles. An added danger lies in the extended breath retention at the end of the exercise. It is recommended that you should break into kumbhaka gradually, by slowly increasing breath retention times from one sitting to the next. Better still is to separately master the two exercises which together constitute Bhastrika. These exercises are Kapalabhati and Ujjayi.

Ujjayi, the Audible Breath

Ujjayi Pranayama consists of a slow, uniform puraka, kumbhaka, and rechaka during which the glottis is kept half closed. This partial closure of the glottis produces an audible sound which probably accounts for the name given to the exercise. *Ujjayi,* or *Uddapi* (by which name it is also called) means "pronounced loudly." There may also be a connection with the Indian greeting, "*Jaya*," or "long life," which is often shouted in exultation.

Ujjayi may be done in any comfortable seat, with your back and neck held erect. Several commentators claim that Ujjayi is the only form of Pranayama which may also be performed standing or even while walking, granted, however, that you do not attempt kumbhaka as you walk.

To practice Ujjayi, inhale air slowly through both nostrils. Contract your throat so as to produce the audible sound from the glottis. As mentioned in chapter 4, this partial closure helps, in the early stages, to regulate the speed and uniformity of the puraka.

When the puraka is complete, close the glottis completely by further contracting your throat. Lower your chin and rest it firmly in the jugular notch in the, by now familiar, Jalandhara Bandha. Hold your breath for two to four times what you took to breathe in. When you are ready, partially reopen the glottis, close your right nostril by pressing on the side of your nose with your thumb, raise your head, and exhale slowly from your left nostril.

One sitting of Ujjayi can consist of anything between 10 and 150 rounds depending on your time and degree of enthusiasm. Normally, 20 rounds of about fifteen seconds each—five minutes in all—will suffice.

The Benefits: The *Gheranda Samhita* is particularly enthusiastic about Ujjayi:

Practice of Ujjayi kumbhaka accomplishes all things. There will be no disorder of phlegm, flatulence or indigestion, rheumatism, consumption, cough, fever or enlarged spleen. A person should master Ujjayi kumbhaka to get rid of old age and death.[6]

This partiality for exaggeration sometimes becomes embarrassing. Nevertheless, Ujjayi does remove phlegm from the throat. It also massages the internal organs, improves digestion, and tones up the respiratory and nervous systems with the consequent advantages to general fitness and health.

Caution: To begin with, kumbhaka should be practiced very briefly, and it should be increased only gradually from one sitting to another. Care must also be taken never to exceed your limits as far as the length of your purakas and rechakas are concerned. Too slow exhalations can result in damage both to your lungs and heart. As mentioned earlier, a sign of overdoing it is when you find yourself gasping for breath or losing control over the speed of subsequent inhalations.

Suryabhedana, the Awakening Sun Breath

Surya, in Sanskrit, means "sun." We have already seen how, in Tantric and Hatha Yogic theory, the sun is equated to the right nostril. Quite logically, therefore, Suryabhedana consists of inhaling through the right nostril in order to awaken (*bhedana*) the coiled serpent power of the Kundalini.

Take a comfortable seat, maintaining your back and head erect, as usual. Holding the third finger of your right hand against the left side of your nose, breathe slowly in through your right nostril. Kumbhaka should follow with both your nostrils closed and your head lowered in the Jalandhara Bandha. Do not release until "pressure is felt right up to the tips of your nails and the roots of your hair."[7] You should then raise your head and exhale slowly through your left nostril.

Actually, it is not advisable to take the kumbhaka this far until you have practiced breath retention often enough to know your own limits. You should aim, therefore, toward a puraka, kumbhaka, rechaka ratio of 1:4:2.

The Benefits: Suryabhedana cleanses the frontal sinuses and tones up the nervous system. It is asserted in the *Hathapradipika* that Suryabhedana also destroys diseases caused by worms,[8] and, in the *Gheranda Samhita*, that it prevents old age, prevents premature death, awakens the Kundalini, and increases the heat of the body.[9]

Caution: Dangers exist only to the extent that one carries breath retention too far. Excessive kumbhaka can cause permanent damage to both the lungs and the heart.

Bhramari, the Bumblebee Breath

This Pranayama exercise takes its name from the sound produced when the uvula and the edge of the soft palate are made to vibrate with the incoming and outgoing breath during puraka and rechaka. Essentially, it's just a question of snoring.

Puraka is performed through both nostrils by means of a fairly rapid expansion of the chest. The soft palate is raised so as to produce a sound resembling the hum of a male bee. Rechaka is done more slowly and the sound emitted is said to resemble the lower hum of the female bee. Kumbhaka may be dispensed with as the goal of the exercise is to make such a sweet and soothing sound that "an indescribable blissful experience fills the minds of eminent Yogis."[10] Few people, however, succeed in producing anything more sublime than a series of rough and irregular grunts. Things do improve with a little practice, although not always sufficiently to convince one to persevere. It helps to try with alternate nostril breathing.

> **The Benefits:** Apart from the production of blissful sounds, Bhramari does clear the nasal passages of phlegm.

> **Caution:** None, as long as you do not inhale too forcibly and for too long.

Sitali, the Cooling Breath

Sitali is one of the only two Pranayama techniques for which puraka is performed by breathing through the mouth.

The tongue is folded lengthwise and made to protrude about half an inch outside the lips. The shape of the tongue forms a tubelike channel with the upper lip. Air should be inhaled through this channel in the normal slow and uniform manner of Pranayama. When the puraka is complete, do kumbhaka with Jalandhara Bandha, then exhale slowly through both nostrils. Ten to twenty rounds should be done in one sitting.

This exercise is more enjoyable in summer than in winter. The effect of sucking the air over a damp tongue cools the body considerably. Hence, the name. *Sital* in Sanskrit, means "cool."

> **The Benefits:** The cooling effect has already been mentioned. According to the *Hathapradipika*, "This kumbhaka, called Sitali, destroys disease like glandular enlargements and disorders of the spleen, fever, disorders of bile, hunger, thirst and poisons."[11] However, these claims have never been investigated scientifically.

> **Caution:** None, as long as kumbhaka is kept within the proper limits.

Sitkari, the Hissing Breath

Sitkari is the other Pranayama technique in which puraka is done through the mouth. The lips are parted over lightly clenched teeth. The tip of the tongue touches the front of the palate, just above the front teeth. Air is then drawn in uniformly with a hissing sound as it passes through the teeth. Kumbhaka may or may not be performed, according to preference. The lips are then closed and rechaka is done normally through both nostrils. Ten to twenty rounds of Sitkari per sitting are adequate.

> **The Benefits:** Svatmarama gets somewhat carried away on this one. He claims in his *Hathapradipika* that:
>
> *By practicing assiduously in this manner, the yogi becomes a second Cupid. He is admired by the whole multitude of yoginis [female yogis]; becomes capable of creating and destroying; and never feels hungry, thirsty, sleepy, or in want of energy. There is no doubt that in this manner the yogi acquires complete control over his body, remains free from all calamities and becomes the most eminent of yogis on the face of the earth.*[12]
>
> However, as far as I know, these claims have never been investigated scientifically, either. The exercise is supposed to give a cooling and thirst quenching effect in summer.
>
> **Caution:** None if practiced properly.

There are two more varieties of Pranayama described in the traditional texts. Neither of these are practiced with any frequency nowadays. They are Moorcha and Plavini.

Moorcha, the Loss of Awareness Breath

Moorcha, in Sanskrit, means "loss of awareness." It is so called because its assiduous practice is supposed to lead to "...loss of awareness and give pleasure."[13]

Commentators put forward various explanations of how this comes about. Some claim that the continuous practice of Jalandhara Bandha (in this exercise the bandha is maintained during rechaka) puts unusual pressure on the carotid artery. The carotid artery is responsible for supplying blood to the brain. If the artery is constrained, blood supply diminishes and unconsciousness results. An alternative though similar explanation makes the carotid sinus responsible. Continuous pressure on this nerve is said to bring about a trancelike sleep.

Others argue that loss of awareness is caused by the cessation of breathing altogether and by the proper use of posture and diet. Yogis have indeed been known to inhibit their respiration to the extent that they go into a trance during which they can be buried underground for days without any harmful effects. Finally, it is suggested that the loss of awareness is brought about simply by the administration of drugs combined with this Pranayama.

Moorcha Pranayama is itself fairly straightforward. Breathe in slowly through both nostrils in the normal manner. When the puraka is complete, adopt a firm Jalandhara Bandha while holding your breath. Exhale slowly without loosening the Jalandhara Bandha chin lock. The appropriate ratio between puraka, kumbhaka, and rechaka is the usual 1:4:2, although yogis bent on entering a trance will lengthen the kumbhaka further. Needless to say, this is not recommended.

> **The Benefits:** A pleasurable trancelike condition during which sensory disturbances are excluded and the mind is left free to concentrate on its spiritual goal. Moorcha also has the usual salutary massaging effects on the internal organs and tones up the nervous system.

> **Caution:** Granted that kumbhaka is kept within the normal limits, no real harm can come of the practice of Moorcha.

Plavini, the Floating Breath

Some confusion exists amongst the authorities as to what Plavini really consists of. *Plavini,* in Sanskrit, means "floating," and is described in the *Hathapradipika* as follows:

> *"With the stomach completely filled with a liberal quantity of air introduced into it, a yogi easily floats like a lotus leaf even in deepest water."*[14]

The word for stomach, udara, is used elsewhere to indicate any bodily cavity. In the *Hathapradipika*, under the description of Bhastrika, the term *yath-udara* specifically means "thoracic cavity," or lungs.[15] Plavini might therefore consist of nothing more than taking a deep breath so as to enable a person to float on water. It must be borne in mind that in medieval India very few people knew how to swim. Being able to float on water would therefore have been considered to be quite a remarkable feat.

If, however, the term *udara* is to be taken literally as meaning "stomach," how does one go about swallowing the air? The technique is referred to in the *Gheranda Samhita* as part of one of Hatha yoga's more abstruse purification techniques called Bahiskrita dhauti.[16] One is instructed to form "the Kaki-mudra and to fill the stomach with air." Forming the Kaki-mudra means taking a mouthful of air, closing the mouth, tightening the cheeks, pursing the lips, and swallowing.

Once the air has been ingested one may then force it out of the stomach by means of two or three long eructations.

Swami Kuvalayananda claims that ordinary Pranayama should be performed with the stomach still full of air, but other commentators argue that this would interfere with the free movement of the diaphragm and the abdominal muscles and might prove dangerous.

> **The Benefits:** Dubious, but before dismissing Plavini altogether, it is only fair to quote Michael Wurmbrand, a physical fitness instructor from Southern California who advocates swallowing breath as a key to health and long life: "Swallowing the breath really works," says Wurmbrand. "It permits air to enter the intestines, where it collects and forms a second source of oxygen for the blood." He claims dramatic results from the three years that he has spent swallowing his breath. "I am forty-nine and as fit as an eighteen-year-old. I can hold my breath for four minutes." He has developed a low resting heart rate and the chest muscles of a weightlifter.[17]
>
> The practice of swallowing air and later eructating it does give some relief in cases of indigestion and chronic gastritis.
>
> **Caution:** Unless you are particularly curious about the effects of ingesting air, it is probably wise to steer clear of Plavini altogether. There is simply too little known about it to make the risk worthwhile. Even Michael Wurmbrand cautions that "much pain and practice are necessary to achieve results." It would therefore seem advisable to wait until more research has been done before adopting this technique on a regular basis.

The exercises discussed are the traditional methods of Pranayama that have been known in India for centuries. Other varieties do exist, although some of them are quite abstruse and practiced only in remote schools of yoga and for purely spiritual ends. The rest consist of minor variations on the exercises that we have described: breathing through one nostril rather than the other, for example, or combining the features of two techniques into one. The advanced student of Pranayama may experiment with any combinations and variations of these basic exercises.

Before experimenting, however, it is wise to be completely confident that you have reached a suitable level of proficiency in the basic Pranayama exercises. On average, at least a year of daily practice is necessary before you can be sure that you have achieved this.

....

....

....

Chapter Six

—

Pranayama
Exercise Programs

There are three reasons for practicing Pranayama: spiritual, curative, and general fitness. There are also three levels of endeavor: intense, medium, and mild, depending on your time, needs, and degree of interest.

For anyone aiming for the mystic experience of Samadhi, the more yoga, meditation, and Pranayama the person does, the better. People with specific ailments can derive a good deal of benefit from a fairly intense practice of Pranayama combined with other exercises and therapies. The ideal, in these cases, is to be able to attend therapy classes where Pranayama is taught by professionals. Such classes are not always easy to find. In the absence of professional help, you might therefore refer to chapter 12 for some information on the appropriate exercises in relation to some common disorders.

For the rest, those with good to average health and an interest in keeping fit, the following daily exercise routines will be adequate.

A FIFTEEN-MINUTE PROGRAM

For those with no time at all, even a mere five minutes of slow deep breathing a day, in the office, in the car, or in the bathroom, is better than nothing at all. But if you do manage to set aside fifteen minutes to keeping fit with Pranayama, the following routine will ensure fitness and health.

1) Start with 30 rounds of Kapalabhati ....30 seconds
(on the last rechaka, exhale completely and adopt)

2) Uddiyana Bandha...30 seconds

3) 1 minute of normal breathing ....1 minute

4) 20 rounds of puraka, kumbhaka, and rechaka ....5-12 minutes
(including Jalandhara Bandha with kumbhaka)   *(depending on kumbhaka)*

5) Complete the session with 2 or 3 minutes of relaxation, breathing normally in one of the meditative poses (Swastikasana, Sukhasana, or Shavasana). Do not allow the mind to wander, keep your attention on the breath as it enters your throat. The ideal, if you meditate regularly, is to complete the session with your normal meditation...2-3 minutes

Total time: 9-17 minutes

A THIRTY-MINUTE PROGRAM

A longer Pranayama program will, of course, allow you greater variety by giving you more time to experiment with different techniques. The ideal amount of time to spend each day on Pranayama would be thirty minutes.

1) Before starting, relax in one of the cross-legged positions ....2 minutes

2) Start with 20 rounds of Bhastrika ....45 seconds

followed by normal breathing ....2 minutes

and another 20 rounds of Bhastrika ....45 seconds

and again, normal breathing, Bhastrika, and finally, 2 more minutes of normal breathing...4 minutes, 45 seconds

3) 30 rounds of Ujjay...7-12 minutes

4) 20 rounds of either Suryabhedana, Sitali, or Sitkari ....5 minutes
(the last two preferably in summer)

5) 5 minutes of relaxation in one of the meditative poses. Concentrate on your breath in your throat...5 minutes

Total time: 32 minutes

THREE COURSES TO CHOOSE FROM

Pranayama sessions of this kind might well be preceded by some active exercises such as Suryanamaskar (Salute to the Sun) or yoga asanas. For more information about these, you should refer to a good illustrated text on Hatha yoga or, better still, to a good yoga school. You will, however, find a brief description of the asanas (positions) mentioned here in the following section.

Three yoga and Pranayama courses practiced at the Kaivalyadhama Institute of Yoga are as follows:

The Full Course for People of Good or Average Health ━━━━━━━━━

1) Shirshasana ....the Head Stand...............................1-12 minutes

2) Sarvangasana ....the Candle Stand ....1-6 minutes

3) Matsyasana ....the Fish ....1-3 minutes

4) Halasana...........................the Plow ....1-5 minutes

5) Bhujangasana ....the Cobra...1-4 minutes
   (3-10 repetitions, each pose maintained for 10-15 seconds)

6) Shalabhasana ....the Locust ....1-4 minutes
   (3-10 repetitions, each pose maintained for 10-15 seconds)

7) Dhanurasana ....the Bow..1-4 minutes
   (3-7 turns, each pose maintained for 10-15 seconds)

8) Ardha-Matsyendrasana ....Spinal Twist ....1-4 minutes

9) Paschimottanasana ....Forward Stretch ....1-2 minutes

10) Shavasana ....the Corpse ....relaxation for 3-10 minutes

11) Uddiyana Bandhha ....1-4 minutes
   (3-7 rounds)

12) Yoga Mudra...1-3 minutes
   (forward bending in cross-legged pose)

13) Kapalabhati ....1-6 minutes
   (3 rounds of 10-120 respirations)

14) Ujjayi Pranayama ....3-10 minutes
   (10-30 rounds)

15) Bhastrika Pranayama...2-7 minutes
   (3 rounds of 10-120 respirations)

Total time: between 20 minutes and 1 hour, 24 minutes *(excluding rests)*

You should start gently and increase the time for each exercise by fifteen to thirty seconds a week. If you are short for time and do not wish to work up to sessions lasting over an hour, it is preferable to attempt one of the Kaivalyadhama Institute's shorter courses rather than rush through the full routine.

The Short Course

1) Bhujangasana ....the Cobra..1-2 minutes
(3 -10 repetitions of each)

2) Shalabhasana ....the Locust ....1-2 minutes
(maintaining the positions for up to 10 seconds)

3) Dhanurasana ....the Bow..1-2 minutes

4) Halasana.........................the Plow...1-2 minutes
(repeat 3-5 times maintaining each final pose for 5 seconds)

5) Paschimottanasana ....Forward Stretch ....1-3 minutes
(3-7 times, maintain the position for 5-15 seconds)

6) Ardha-Matsyendrasana.....Spinal Twist ....1-3 minutes
(3-7 times, maintain the final position for 5 seconds)

7) Uddiyana Bandha..2-3 minutes
(3-5 times, maintain the bandha for 10-15 seconds)

8) Ujjayi Pranayama ....2-3 minutes
(10-20 rounds)

Total time: 8-20 minutes (excluding rests)

If you find exercises like Uddiyana Bandha, Dhanurasana, Pachimottanasana, or Ardha-Matsyendrasana too strenuous, you might prefer to start with the easy course first. In the sequence of exercises, Ujjayi Pranayama is followed by positions which, although quite difficult to perform properly, can still be beneficial even when incompletely executed. A Halasana-Plow position which does not bring the legs to the floor above the head still stretches the spinal column and hamstrings. Bhujangasana—the Cobra—need not stretch back all the way to exert is effects. Shalabhasana—the Locust—strengthens the lumbar region even when the feet are raised but a few inches. Chakrasana—the Wheel—need not, of course, be practiced in its more difficult form; the easier version (see figure 29) is envisaged here.

The Easy Course

1) Ujjayi Pranayama ....3-5 minutes
(7-14 rounds)

2) Halasana............................the Plow ....45-90 seconds
(3-6 turns, hold the final position 2 seconds)

3) Bhujangasana ....the Cobra ....30-75 seconds
(2-5 times, maintaining each pose for 5 seconds)

4) Shalabhasana ....the Locust ....30-75 seconds
(2-5 repetitions, hold each pose for 5 seconds)

5) Vrikshanasana ....One-Legged Stand ....45-90 seconds
(3-6 times, maintain 5 seconds for each leg)

6) Chakrasana.......................the Wheel....................................30-75 seconds
(2-5 bends, keep each position for 2 seconds)

Total time: 6-13 minutes *(excluding rests)*

There is no reason why Pranayama cannot usefully be combined with exercises of a more strenuous nature. Pranayama may be performed either before or after the rest of your fitness routine, depending on your goals. If you want to end the whole program peacefully with a sense of balance and calm well-being, yoga and Pranayama exercises are best done last. If, on the other hand, you wish to train your lungs first and end the program with a sense of exhilaration, do Pranayama first and your running, jumping, weight lifting, or whatever, afterward.

At least twenty minutes must always elapse between any strenuous exercise routine and your yoga-Pranayama.

Chapter Seven

—

Yoga Asanas:
Hatha Yoga Positions

Several Hatha yoga postures have been mentioned in the previous chapter as corollary exercises to the Pranayama techniques described therein. (Rather than refer to a separate text on the subject of yoga asanas, the editors chose to describe these positions here.) Much the same rules exist concerning time, place, and dress for the practice of Yoga asanas as for that of Pranayama. You should, therefore, try to perform your asanas regularly, at the same time each day. You should dress lightly, the lighter the better, but beware of catching cold in winter.

Your yoga asanas must be performed on an empty stomach. Allow at least two and a half hours after a meal and half an hour after a glass of water. Do not eat until at least half an hour has elapsed after finishing your asanas.

Asanas should be performed on a hard, even surface—on a thick rug or a folded blanket placed on the floor. Do not try them on a soft mattress or on a bed, you simply won't be able to hold the postures steadily enough.

Your room should be well ventilated or, weather permitting, you might choose to practice your yoga outdoors.

You should go into your asanas feeling relaxed. Shower beforehand if this helps. You should choose as quiet an environment as possible. Silence promotes concentration on the actual movements and positions. Do *not* listen to music. No matter how mellow, music will distract.

You should be reasonably fit when you start doing asanas. Beware of overexerting yourself at the outset. Never force your body beyond what you feel are its natural limits. Do your best though. Even if your positions are only half complete, do not worry. Practice makes perfect. After a month or two you will find yourself slipping into most of the postures with ease.

Women should not practice yoga asanas during their menstrual periods and after the fourth month of pregnancy.

Yoga asanas should be performed slowly with two or three minutes rest in Shavasana between each position.

Shirshasana: The Head Stand

The beginner may find it easier to perform this position against a wall. Many people are inhibited by the prospect of overbalancing without a wall to lean against. You may also like to place a soft cushion under your head for the sake of comfort.

Kneel on the ground and interlock your fingers, as if you were about to pray. Place your hands on the floor in front of you with your open palms toward you. Keeping your fingers interlocked, put your head against your palms. Lift your knees off the floor and shuffle your feet slowly forward until you are firmly balanced on the top of your head and elbows. Now breathe in through your nostrils, hold your breath, raise your feet off the floor, and gradually straighten your body until your head and feet are in a straight vertical line.

You should hold the position for twenty to thirty seconds to begin with. Later three or four minutes can be maintained with ease. Breathe normally through your nose while in the head stand.

Lower your body to the ground gradually and do not raise your head at once as this may make you dizzy. Relax for a few minutes with your head on your hands before sitting up straight.

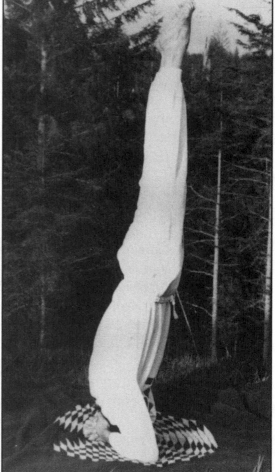

Figure 17: Shirshasana, the Head Stand

The Benefits: A richer flow of blood to the brain, eyes, neck, and ears while easing pressure on the heart. The spinal column is strengthened. The lumbar and sacral part of the vertebral column, which normally carries the weight of the whole upper body, is relieved of pressure. Shirshasana is said to improve one's mental powers and to banish gray hair. It is useful for people suffering from varicose veins or grey hair.

Caution: Not advisable for anybody suffering from abnormally high blood pressure. Make sure that the weight of the body is on the elbows and on the *top* of your head. Weight on your forehead can twist and damage the cervical vertebra.

Never stand up immediately after the head stand. A sudden return to a standing position puts undue effort on the heart and can lead to blackouts.

Sarvangasana: The Candle Stand

Lie on your back with feet together and arms by your sides, your palms flat against the floor. Breathe in and raise your legs together until they are at right angles to the rest of your body. Keep your legs straight throughout. Exhale. Inhale, bring your legs back over your head and raise your hips and trunk until your body is straight and the tips of your toes are directly above your eyes. You may, if you wish, support your back with your hands. Your chest should be pressing against your chin. Breathe normally when the position has been attained. You should keep it for as long as you feel comfortable up to a maximum of five minutes. Lower your body by repeating the same sequence of movements in reverse. Rest in the Shavasana position for at least two minutes before continuing.

The Benefits: Sarvangasana is said to have a beneficial effect on the endocrine glands, especially the thyroid. It stretches the spinal column and the muscles of the back, neck, and legs. It tones up the abdominal muscles, removes constipation and gastric problems, improves digestion, and reduces excess fat. It increases the circulation of blood to the brain and exercises the bronchi and the lungs.

Caution: As with Shirshasana, it's not advisable for anyone suffering from hypertension or damaged cervical vertebra.

Sarvangasana should be followed by a backward bending position such as Matsyasana which exercises the parts of the neck and shoulders left inactive during Sarvangasana.

Figure 18 A & B: Sarvangasana, the Candle Stand

Matsyasana: The Fish Posture

Matsyasana is best performed in the Lotus pose (Padmasana). If you find this difficult, the alternative position is to lie on your back with your knees together and bent so as to allow your heels to press against your buttocks. Place your hands under your thighs. Breathe in and arch your back while supporting yourself on your elbows and pulling on your thighs. When you have arched your back as far as possible, rest the weight of your upper body on your elbows and head Maintain the position for ten to fifteen seconds at first, for thirty seconds later. Breathe slowly and deeply through your nostrils.

Return to your resting position by pulling on your thighs, raising your head slightly, and supporting your body on your elbows. Rest for the space of four or five normal breaths before repeating the posture twice more.

If you are able to perform Matsyasana from the Lotus pose, the entire sequence is exactly the same as that described above except that you should hold onto your feet or the front of your thighs rather than using the back of your thighs as a support.

> **The Benefits:** It corrects the disorders of the respiratory system by expanding the lungs and the bronchi. The neck, chest, vertebral column, and stomach also benefit. This exercise is particularly useful for removing stiffness from the cervical and lumbar regions of the spine. It stretches the muscles of the abdomen and strengthens those of the back. A salutary influence is exerted on the thyroid glands.
>
> **Caution:** There are no real dangers. Care should be taken, however, not to force oneself into the position. Without practice, it is possible to pull the muscles of the back and thighs.

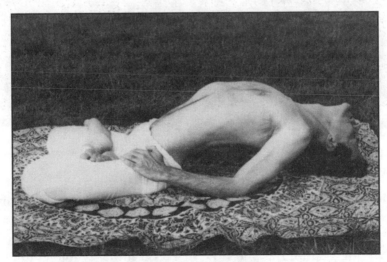

Figure 19: Matsyasana, the Fish posture

Halasana: The Plow Posture

Probably the finest of all the asanas, Halasana, the Plow, is performed from the same starting position as Sarvangasana, or the Candle Stand. Lie on you back with your legs straight and feet touching, your arms along your sides. Breathe in and raise your legs together until your legs are at right angles to the floor. Exhale. Inhale and bring your feet above your head. Do not straighten your body completely. Find your balance and exhale. Inhale then exhale slowly as you lower your feet toward the ground behind your head. Touch the ground with your toes and breathe normally. When you are comfortable take small steps away from your head in order to stretch your spine further. Your legs should be straight and your knees together throughout the exercise. Maintain the position for as long as you feel comfortable. Fifteen seconds will suffice to begin with. With practice, you should be able to keep it for about five minutes.

In order to return to your starting position, raise your feet from the ground and unroll your vertebra while keeping your knees as close to your face as you can.

Your movements should be slow and controlled throughout. Adopt the Shavasana resting position for at least one minute after Halasana.

Figure 20: Halasana, the Plow

The Benefits: Halasana exercises every inch of the spinal column rendering it flexible and youthful. It eliminates abnormal growth and sedimentary mineral deposits from the vertebra. It improves the flow of blood in the whole column. It tones up the nervous system and the sexual glands in both men and women. It exercises the abdominal and back muscles and is said to rejuvenate the entire body. Circulation is improved by regular practice.

Caution: Not suitable for people suffering from defects or damage to the spinal column. As in all asanas, it is important never to force the full position immediately. Bring your legs slowly toward the ground over your head. Do not touch the ground with your toes or straighten your legs completely until you feel perfectly comfortable.

Bhujangasana: The Cobra

Bhujangasana is usually performed immediately after Halasana in order to exert equal and opposite pressure on the spine and back muscles.

Lie on your stomach with your forehead on the ground and the flat of your hands against the floor directly under your shoulders. Your elbows should be folded close to your body. Keep your legs straight and heels together.

Breathe in and slowly tilt your head backward and then raise your chest off the floor. Do not support yourself with your hands until this becomes absolutely necessary to continue lifting your trunk away from the ground. In the final position, the whole of your upper torso should be raised off the floor while your navel should still be touching the ground. You should be looking at the ceiling. Breathe normally for five to ten seconds before lowering your body to the floor. Rest for the space of four or five breaths before repeating another twice.

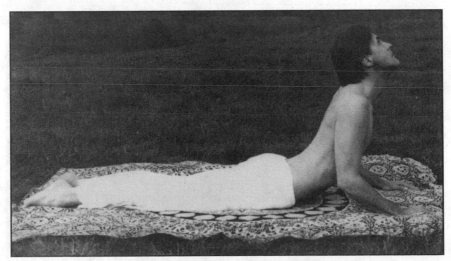

Figure 21: Bhujangasana, the Cobra

The Benefits: Tones the muscles of the back, stretches the abdominal muscles, and massages the whole area thus strengthening the pancreas, liver, and the digestive organs. It is regarded as one of the best remedies for constipation, indigestion, stomachache, and diarrhea. It can relieve menstrual irregularities and exerts a powerful tonic effect on the ovaries and uterus. It also increases the flexibility of the spine, corrects bad posture, and improves the efficiency of the nervous system.

Caution: This is an easy exercise to perform and does not entail any particularly dangerous movement. As always, never strain beyond your limits.

Shalabhasana, The Locust Position

Lie on your stomach with your closed fists between your pelvis bones and the floor. Rest your chin on the ground and breathe in. Holding your breath, use your lower back muscles to raise both legs together toward the ceiling. Hold for a few seconds. Lower your legs and exhale. Rest and repeat twice.

This exercise may also be performed with less exertion by raising one leg at a time rather than both together.

The Benefits: The Locust pose strengthens the lower back muscles. It improves posture and benefits the abdominal area.

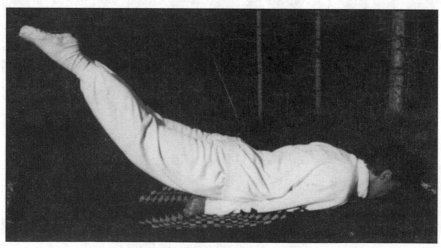

Figure 22: Shalabasana, the Locust

Caution: Raise your legs slowly. This posture puts strain on muscles in the lower back which are rarely exercised. Sudden leg raising without previous practice can pull and damage these muscles.

Dhanurasana: The Bow Posture

The Bow posture is one of the best backward stretching exercises available.

Lie on your stomach. Grasp your ankles and pull on them to raise your thighs and trunk as far off the ground as possible. Exhale before you begin to arch your body and inhale when you have achieved the bow position. Hold the pose for ten to fifteen seconds before returning to your resting position. To begin with it is admissible to keep your knees apart, but try, if you can, to keep them as close as possible. Eventually, they should be touching throughout the asana. Rest for a few seconds before repeating twice.

The Benefits: Dhanurasana has a curative effect on the joints, spine, chest, lungs, and abdomen. It corrects menstrual and other problems related to the reproductive organs in women. It tones up the nervous and endocrine systems and is said to be particularly useful in maintaining a healthy pancreas. It also corrects postural defects.

Figure 23: Dhanurasana, the Bow

Ardha-Matsyendrasana: The Spinal Twist

A complicated position, but easier to perform than it looks or sounds.

Sit on the floor with your legs stretched before you. Bend your left knee and place your left heel against your perineum. Raise your right knee and place your right foot on the floor to the *left* of your left knee. Now twist your torso in such a way as to be able to grasp your right ankle with your left hand with your left arm *outside* your right knee. Your free right hand should be on the floor behind you, bent across your back with the fingers pointing away from you. Exhale and twist your torso as far round as you are able to. Hold the position for five seconds. Inhale and return. Repeat the asana in the opposite direction.

If you find this difficult either to follow or to do, try it another way.

Sit as in the initial position, above. Place your right hand on the floor behind you. Raise your right knee and place your foot on the floor to the right of your left knee. Place your left hand on the ground on the outside of your right knee. The back of your upper arm should be pressed against your knee. Now exert pressure with your left hand against the ground as you twist your trunk round to the right. Return to your starting position and repeat to the other side.

Figure 24: Ardha-Matsyendrasana, the Spinal Twist

The Benefits: Tones up the nervous, endocrine, and digestive systems. It is said to correct disorders of the kidneys, spleen, liver, intestines, bladder, stomach, and sexual organs. It also removes rigidity from the spine by toning the spinal nerve roots and supplying the ligaments and vertebra with plenty of blood. It gives relief from lumbago and muscular rheumatism of the back.

Caution: None if practiced without straining.

Paschimottanasana: The Forward Stretch

Sit on the floor with your legs stretched directly in front of you. Both your heels and your toes should be touching. Your trunk should be straight and your hands resting on the floor next to your thighs.

Exhale and slowly stretch your arms and upper body toward your toes. Grasp your big toes with the corresponding hands—if you can't reach, hold your ankles instead—and bow your head toward your knees. In the completed posture your legs should still be absolutely straight, your head should rest on your knees, and your elbows should touch the floor. If you find this impossible, not to worry. Just stretch as far as you can without bending your legs. Maintain the position for a few seconds, inhale, and straighten your body. Rest for five to ten seconds and repeat.

> **The Benefits:** Paschimottanasana stretches the muscles of the leg and rejuvenates the spinal column. It can cure postural defects, relieve digestive problems and stomach problems, normalize the functioning of the nervous system, and regulate the endocrine system. Its effect on the pancreas is said activate the secretion of insulin in diabetics. Its immediate and most obvious effect is to pull on the hamstring, thereby strengthening it.
>
> **Caution:** Take care if you suffer from severe back problems. Best results are obtained if the legs are kept straight throughout the exercise.

Figure 25 A & B: Paschimottanasana, the Forward Stretch

Yoga Mudra: The Symbol of Yoga

The Yoga Mudra—the symbol of yoga—is best performed in the Lotus posture, or Padmasana. If you find this difficult, any other cross-legged seated position will do.

Take your seat and bring your arms behind your back, gripping one of your wrists with the opposite hand. Close your free hand into a fist.

Breathe deeply and gently for a minute or two before exhaling and simultaneously slowly lowering your body as far forward as you are able to. Your exhalation should be complete just as your forehead touches the floor. If you find this difficult, do not worry. Don't strain your back; just reach as far forward as feels comfortable. Now hold your breath, tighten the grip on your wrist, and gradually raise your arms behind you until they are perpendicular to the rest of your body. Maintain the position for five to ten seconds without breathing.

Inhale while lowering your arms. Raise your trunk and return to your starting position. Relax for twenty to thirty seconds before repeating twice more.

> **The Benefits:** Yoga Mudra exercises the lungs and the bronchi and stimulates blood circulation in the upper torso. It corrects postural defects, removes gastric and digestive problems, cures constipation, and is said to enhance sexual potency.
>
> **Caution:** None if practiced on an empty stomach and without straining.

Figure 26: Yoga Mudra, the symbol of yoga

Vrikshanasana: The Tree Pose

Stand straight with your feet together and your arms hanging loosely by your sides.

Lift your right leg off the floor, bend your knee and, with the help of your hands, place the outside of your right foot against your left thigh. To aid balancing, keep your eyes fixed on one spot in front of you. When you feel comfortable and well balanced, straighten your arms and raise your hands slowly sideways from your body to the top of your head. Join your palms together resting the wrists on your head. Maintain the position for about ten seconds. In one variation of the position, you may, if you wish, straighten your arms above your head while keeping your palms together. Return to your starting position by going through this sequence in reverse, and repeat with your left foot against your right thigh. Breathe normally throughout.

Figure 27: Vrikshanasana, the Tree position

The Benefits: This asana activates most of the major joints in the body. It tones up the muscles in the legs, arms, and shoulders and improves blood circulation. Particularly good for arthritis and joint pains. A good balance-enhancing exercise as well.

Caution: Always practice on a smooth flat surface and away from objects you do not wish to fall (or hop) over if getting into the position proves difficult.

Chakrasana: The Wheel

A difficult posture which requires a good deal of athletic prowess to perform.

Lie on your back with your knees bent and your heels against your buttocks. Your arms should be bent at the elbows and your hands on the floor at either side of your head. Your fingers must be pointing toward your shoulders.

Press your hands and feet firmly against the ground. Take a deep breath and push your whole body upward until you form a full arch. Maintain for as long as you can hold your breath. Gently return to your starting position. Rest for thirty to sixty seconds and repeat twice more.

> **The Benefits:** Chakrasana strengthens the spine and the muscles of the back, arms, and legs. It prevents and alleviates digestive problems and stomach problems and tones up the nervous system.

> **Caution:** Do not overexert yourself in order to achieve the full position or you may pull a muscle.

If the full Chakrasana seems too difficult, an easier version of the Wheel posture does exist.

Kneel, raise your buttocks, and bend slowly backward while grasping your ankles. Arch your body forward as far as you are able. Hold your breath in the position for five to ten seconds. Return to kneeling. Repeat three times.

Figure 28: Chakrasana, the Wheel (full position)

Figure 29: Chakrasana, the Wheel (easy pose)

Ekpada Uttanasana: Single Leg Raising

Lie on your back with your legs straight, heels together, and your arms by your sides, palms downward.

Stretch the toes of your right leg, tighten the muscles, inhale, and then slowly raise your leg until it is at right angles to your body. Maintain the position for as long as you can hold your breath. Exhale. Inhale and then lower your leg to the starting position. Rest for fifteen seconds and repeat with the other leg. Repeat the sequence three to five times at a sitting.

> **The Benefits:** This exercises gives elasticity to the hip joint, strengthens the abdominal muscles, and tones up the digestive system and reproductive systems. The retention of breath during the exercise activates the linings of the bronchi.
>
> **Caution:** This exercise presents no dangers.

Uttanpadasana: Two Leg Raising

The above exercise may be performed by raising both legs together. In this case it is called Uttanpadasana. It affords the same benefits as the single leg raising form albeit in a more "concentrated" form. Raising both legs together entails greater exertion than single leg raising and should, therefore, be practiced only after the simpler asana has been mastered.

Figure 30: Ekpada Uttanasana, single leg raising

Figure 31: Uttanpadasana, two leg raising

Figures 32, 33 & 34: Tarasana, the Star position

Tarasana: The Star

This exercise consists of holding your breath as you put your hands and arms through four different motions. Your body should be held straight throughout.

Begin by standing straight with your feet about six inches apart and at right angles to one another. Let your arms hang loosely at your sides. Look straight ahead.

1) Straighten your fingers and hold your palms forward. Slowly inhale as you raise your arms forward until they reach shoulder level and are parallel to the floor. Hold your breath and keep your arms straight and firm with your palms upward. Keep this position for a second or two.

2) While still holding your breath, turn your palms toward the floor and move your arms outward until they are in a straight line with your shoulders. Pause for a second.

3) Bring your arms forward and once again parallel to one another. Turn your outstretched palms toward one another and raise your arms skyward. Maintain for a second or two.

4) Turn your palms outward and lower your arms until they are in a straight line with your shoulders and parallel to the floor (the same position as in 2). Hold for a second before exhaling and slowly lowering your arms back to your starting position at your sides.

Take four or five slow, deep breaths before repeating the sequence twice more.

The Benefits: Tarasana exercises the chest, lungs, and the bronchi and is thus particularly valid for asthmatics. It also develops the chest, arm, and shoulder muscles.

Caution: None.

Pawanmuktasana: The Wind Liberating Position

Pawan, in Sanscrit, means "air" or "wind." *Mukta* means "liberating." Hence this specific position against air in the intestines. The asana may be performed either standing or lying. In the text it is recommended for heart patients; in which case, the lying position is to be preferred.

Lie on your back with your arms by your sides. Inhale and pull your right knee up toward your chest. Hold your ankle lightly with your right hand and pull your knee toward you with your left hand. Exhale as you pull. Raise your head so as to touch your knee with your forehead. Maintain the position for about ten seconds. Release and return to your starting position.

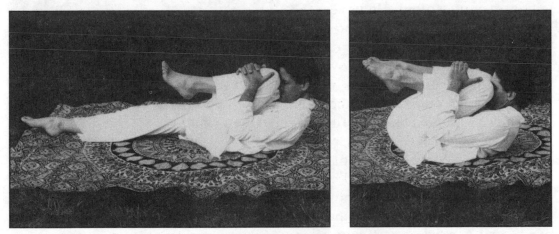

Figure 35 A & B: Pawanmuktasana, the Wind Liberating pose

Repeat with your left leg. The sequence may be repeated from three to six times at a sitting.

Pawanmuktasana may also be performed with both legs together. In this case, pull on each knee with the corresponding hand.

> **The Benefits:** This asana activates the pancreas and the abdominal organs. It helps relieve intestinal gasses and indigestion, loosens the hip joints, and is said to cure constipation.

> **Caution:** None if performed lying down. Balance will be maintained more easily in the vertical version of this position by standing on a flat, even surface and by fixing your gaze on a single spot.

Gomukhasana: The Cow Posture

So called because the contortions of both arms and legs in this position is supposed to look like the face of a cow. *Gomukhasana,* in Sanskrit, means "cow."

This asana may be performed by simply kneeling on the ground and sitting on your ankles (your toes should be touching and your ankles apart so you are, in fact, sitting on the inner sides of your soles). However, the formal position is a little more complicated. You should kneel on one leg only and cross the other leg over the opposite thigh. Bring the heel of your crossed leg as close to your body as possible. You should be sitting (uncomfortably) on one ankle.

Having adopted this position, slowly fold your left elbow and bring it behind your back. Your fingers should be stretched upward and the back of your hand pressed against your spine.

Figure 36: Gomukhasana, the Cow posture

Now bend your right arm over your right shoulder and stretch so that the fingers of each hand touch. If you can manage it, hook the fingers of your two hands together. When your fingers are firmly gripping one another, pull upward as far as you can with your right arm. Your spine should be straight at all times. Maintain the position for ten seconds, loosen your finger grip, and return to your starting position. Rest your hands on your thighs. Breathe normally for twenty to thirty seconds and repeat the exercise on the opposite side of the body.

> **The Benefits:** Gomukhasana exercises the major and minor joints of the hands, arms, ankles, and legs, rendering them flexible and removing any excess synovial fluid which may be present. It prevents bursitis, that is the formation of calcium deposits in the shoulder joints. It also strengthens the lungs and heart as well as the muscles of the chest and arms.

> **Caution:** Care must be taken not to sprain ankles or knee joints. Place the weight of your body on your hands before shifting to your ankles. The complete position with the weight of the body on one ankle is not recommended for people of exceptional size and body weight. If this is the case place your ankles by your buttocks, with your toes facing outward, not under them.

Shavasana: The Corpse Posture

Shavasana is the ideal resting position between asanas and at the beginning or end of a yoga sitting. It has a relaxing effect on the whole body and should be practiced with frequency by anybody suffering from heart or circulatory problems.

Lie on your back with your feet about nine inches apart and your hands at your sides at about four inches from the body. Your toes should point slightly outward and your hands should be resting on their side with the fingers slightly bent.

Close your eyes and breathe slowly and deeply with your abdomen. You may, if you wish, practice Nei Dan Qi Gong in this position.

Another relaxation technique is to concentrate on each of the muscles of your fingers and hands in turn. Isolate each muscle by imagining that you are about to move it, but relax it instead. Do this with your left hand then your right, your left forearm, your right, your biceps and your shoulders. Then start with your feet and work up the whole body. Your limbs should feel absolutely relaxed and like a dead weight against the floor. Finish off with your facial muscles. Because of the enormous number of muscles in the face, it pays to relax this part of the body twice. The entire relaxation sequence should take no longer than ten minutes.

The Benefits: Very relaxing. To be practiced frequently by anyone suffering from hypertension or heart and circulatory problems. It is particularly effective for combating insomnia. If you can't sleep just roll over on your back and try Shavasana while concentrating on each muscle as described above.

Caution: Take care not to fall asleep, unless, of course, you want to!

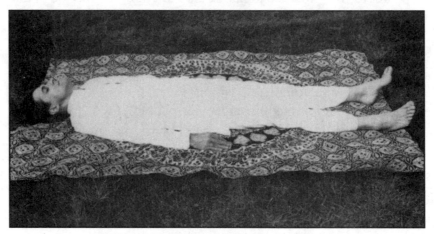

Figure 37: Shavasana, the Corpse posture

Chapter Eight
—
Qi Gong

Qi Gong differs from Pranayama in that more is expected of it.

The Chinese believe that through correct breathing techniques, Qi may be accumulated in the abdomen and subsequently made to circulate through the whole body, ensuring health and eventually giving one the power to heal others.

In theory, during Nei Dan, or inner Qi Gong (the literal meaning is "internal elixir"), the mind focuses the incoming Qi on the Dan Tian, the center of all bodily energy situated in the lower abdomen. The abdominal muscles are strengthened by the breathing exercises and more energy is generated. When sufficient Qi has accumulated in the Dan Tian, the mind directs this energy through the two major Qi channels, the Ren Mei channel; and Du Mei, which are said to be situated at the front and back of the torso respectively. This is called the "Small Circulation" of Qi, or Xiao Zhou Tian. Later, when an even greater amount of Qi is present, this is made to flow through all twelve energy channels in the body in what is known as the Da Zhou Tian or "Grand Circulation." It is said to result in perfect fitness and health. The first step in the above exercise is correct abdominal breathing.

THE POSTURE

Although Padmasana is not generally practiced in China, any of the cross-legged positions used for Pranayama are suitable for the initial stage of Nei Dan Qi Gong. It is argued that while endeavoring to circulate the Qi around the torso (in the Small Circulation exercise) it is useful to keep the legs crossed. Crossed legs partially obstruct the entrance to the lower channels in the legs thus ensuring that the accumulated Qi does not go shooting off in the wrong direction. Later, when the Grand Circulation is attempted, a standing pose will become necessary.

The Standing Position

Stand with your feet shoulder-width apart, toes pointing slightly inward. Bend your knees slightly as if you were about to take a seat. The weight of your body should be on your feet and lower legs, not on your thigh muscles. Imagine that there are ants running around under your heels. This helps distribute your weight properly with your heels on the ground but all your weight on the balls of your feet. Hold your back and neck straight and raise your arms, bending them at the elbows, as if to encircle a large balloon. Your fingers should be splayed in this same balloon encircling position. Do not raise your shoulders. Your body should feel relaxed and comfortable.

Figure 38: Qi Gong standing position

The Benefits: This position is Qi Gong's most important pose. All Qi circulatory exercises can be done in the standing position. In the opinion of many teachers, this pose is the only one a student of Qi Gong need learn and practice. The benefits appear to be all those derivable from Qi Gong as a whole (see chapter 2, page 20). In the short term, this position strengthens the muscles of the back, legs, arms, and abdomen.

Caution: Do not overexert yourself in the beginning. The position looks easy but, because of the unusual angle of the legs, a good deal of strain is put on the thighs as well as the arms. Ten minutes of this position can leave one feeling quite weak. Increase your time in the position gradually.

Supine Positions

Two lying positions are envisaged in Qi Gong exercises. The first is simply to lie on your back with your head on a pillow, arms by your sides and legs extended. Keep your eyes, mouth, and teeth closed. Press the tip of your tongue against your palate. This position is to be employed for relaxation. Starting with your toes, and moving up your legs, followed by your hands, arms, torso, and face, relax each part of the body, and each muscle in sequence. Breathe slowly, deeply, and evenly through your nose.

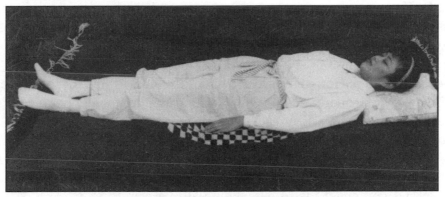

Figure 39: Qi Gong lying position

The second lying position is on your right side. Your right arm should be bent and resting on a pillow next to your head. This posture is used in Qi Gong for elementary breath retention and relaxation. Breath retention of three to seven seconds is suggested after each exhalation. This should give a minimum of stimulus to the Dan Tian energy center in the abdomen.

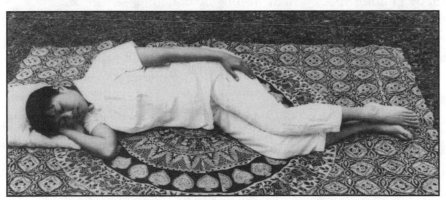

Figure 40: Qi Gong lying position

Nei Dan, Xiao Zhou Tian: Small Circulation Abdominal Breathing

Two methods of abdominal breathing exist for Xiao Zhou Tian, or Small Circulation. They are the Buddhist and the Taoist breathing techniques. Both envisage a cross-legged seated pose although, with experience, they may also be done in the Standing pose (see page 92).

The Buddhist technique consists of focusing on the abdomen while breathing slowly and uniformly through your nostrils. Expand your abdomen as you breathe in, contract it as you breathe out. Do not hold your breath.

The Taoist technique is more common and is the opposite of the Buddhist. You concentrate on your abdomen, as above, but you must contract it when you inhale and expand it when you exhale. Taoist breathing also goes by the name of Fan Hu Xi, or reverse breathing.

Abdominal expansion should never be forced, but should be perfected gradually, with gentle daily practice, until you learn to expand it from your navel to your pubic bone.

Once this has been achieved, you should sit in quiet meditation, concentrating on your breathing. Feel, or imagine, the breath traveling from your nose to the Dan Tian in your abdomen. You should imagine it rather as if you were swallowing something and you could feel it descending all the way to your navel. After a few sittings, you should begin to feel a tingling sensation and warmth in the abdominal area. This means that your Qi has accumulated sufficiently and that you are now ready to attempt the Xiao Zhou Tian (Small Circulation). This is done by guiding the Qi around your torso with your mind. It is said, in China, that wherever the mind goes, the Qi follows. At first it will only be a question of imagination and a little Qi. With time, however, the flow of Qi will become stronger and thus more perceptible.

Begin by guiding your Qi in the following breathing sequence:

1) Close your mouth and eyes. Press your tongue against your palate. Inhale and guide the incoming Qi from your nose to the Dan Tian. Tighten your sphincter muscles during the inhalation.
2) Exhale and guide the Qi from the Dan Tian through the groin and into the abdominal cavity located in the coccyx, or tailbone. This is called the Wei Lu cavity. Relax your sphincter as you exhale.
3) Inhale and guide the Qi to the base of your neck, between your shoulders.

4) During the final exhalation, guide the Qi from the back of your neck to your ears then down to your nose and mouth. When the Qi enters your mouth relax your tongue from its position against the roof of your mouth.

One full cycle of Xiao Zhou Tian thus includes two respirations.

You should continue the Small Circulation exercise for ten minutes two or three times a day. After three months of regular practice you should be ready to go on to the Grand Circulation exercise.

The Benefits: All those deriving from Qi Gong practice as a whole. Extremely beneficial to the lungs, abdominal viscera, heart, and nervous system.

Caution: None.

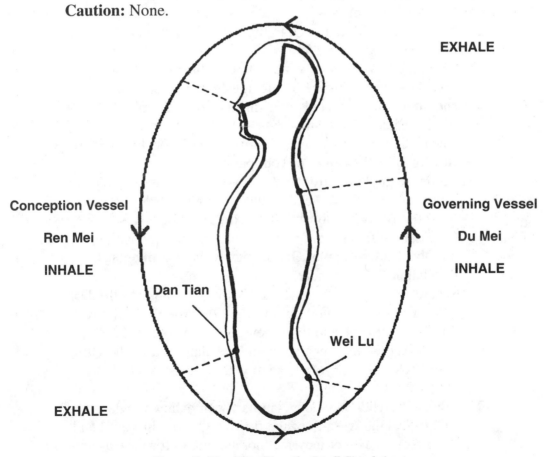

Figure 41: Xiao Zhou Tian, the Small Circulation

Da Zhou Tian: The Grand Circulation Exercise

You are ready to go on to the Da Zhou Tian only when you are confident that you are able to circulate Qi around your torso. Evidence that you are able to do this correctly consists of a feeling of warmth in all the areas of your body through which your Qi is being guided by your mind.

Your pose for the first phase of the Grand Circulation technique should be either sitting in a chair or standing, preferably in the Qi Gong standing position (see page 92).

1) Breathe in while contracting your abdomen (or expanding it, if you prefer the Buddhist method of respiration). Guide the Qi from your nose to the Dan Tian. Tighten the sphincter muscles.

2) Exhale and guide the Qi to the Wei Lu in the coccyx. Relax your sphincter muscles.

3) Inhale while guiding the Qi to the back of your neck, between the shoulders.

4) During the final exhalation do not guide the Qi over the top of your head to your nose as previously, but direct it from the shoulders to your hands and fingers. Your thumb and little finger should be touching.

5) Repeat the cycle over several sittings until you feel a warm flow of Qi to the center of your palms.

6) In order to guide the flow of Qi to your lower limbs the usual procedure is followed except that you should adopt a supine position. By lying down and relaxing your leg muscles, the Qi is said to flow with greater ease. A standing position will not obstruct the flow of Qi completely, but simply constrains the channels a little more.

7) Breathe in as usual, guiding the Qi from the nose to the Dan Tian. Exhale and, now, guide the Qi through your groin, through your legs, and to the center of your soles.

8) On your subsequent inhalation and exhalation, take the Qi up your back and over your head to your nose as usual.

The Benefits: The Da Zhou Tian has been achieved when you are able to feel the warmth of the flowing Qi both in your hands and your feet. Your feet may feel hot and numb for several days after you have successfully directed your Qi to them. However, do not expect results too quickly. It can take years, and a minimum of six months to circulate your Qi successfully to your hands and feet.

Later, you will be able to guide the Qi to both your hands and feet simultaneously. You will be able to direct the Qi to any part of your body at will. You will be able to cure your ailments. You will be able to expand your Qi beyond your own body, transmitting it to others thereby healing their illnesses. Or so it is said.

Caution: If there is any truth to the theory that one can cure other people's illnesses by the laying on of hands, one is advised not to attempt this without expert guidance. If it works, the beginner is said not to be able to stop the Qi flowing out of his body thus leading to Qi exhaustion. It is also argued that taking in outside Qi risks Qi incompatibility and negative energy influences.

STRENGTHENING QI

After you have successfully controlled the Small and the Grand Circulations of Qi around your body, you may wish to take things further by increasing the strength of your Qi.

Several exercises have been developed in China to these ends. Many of these are used for martial arts training and involve concentrating Qi in specific parts of the body such as the palms of the hand or the fingers. Sufficient literature exists on the martial arts to dispense with a study of these techniques in the present context. In any case, the methods in question have no immediate bearing on breathing for health purposes. We shall, therefore, examine only three exercises for training the Qi that are based on breath control. Two of these exercises will be accomplished more easily after you have learned the Grand Circulation method. There is no reason why you cannot practice the third from the very start, while you are still concentrating on the Xiao Zhou Tian, or Small Circulation.

Lian Qi

Lian Qi, in Sanscrit, means nothing more complicated than "training the Qi."

When you are confident that you have mastered the Da Zhou Tian technique, you may further reinforce your breathing by narrowing the glottis and making lighter inhalations.

Adopt the Qi Gong standing pose. Contract your throat and inhale lightly while expanding your abdomen. Exhale immediately you have finished inhaling. Your breathing should be faster and shallower than previously.

After about three months of steady practice (five minutes a day is an adequate amount of time), you should try to dispense with thoracic breathing altogether. Your abdominal movements should now be slower and less perceptible. This exercise requires a great deal of tranquillity and attentiveness.

> **The Benefits:** Abdominal massage, strengthening of the nervous system, and increased control over your Qi.

> **Caution:** None if performed correctly.

Breath Retention Exercise

Take either a seated or a supine position, close your eyes, and direct your attention to the Dan Tian in your abdomen. Inhale slowly and uniformly using the whole of your lungs. Imagine the Qi descending to the Dan Tian. When your inhalation is complete, draw in your abdomen and hold your breath for thirty seconds. Exhale slowly and without effort.

The exercise should be repeated for fifteen or twenty minutes and may gradually be extended up to an hour. Chinese Qi Gong masters suggests that, after some months of practice, breath retention may be made to last for as long as two minutes. In no circumstances, however, must you rush the exhalation or gasp for air during the subsequent inhalation.

> **The Benefits:** Breath retention provides effective abdominal massage and tones up the nervous system.

> **Caution:** All breath retention exercises can be harmful to both the heart and the lungs when the breath is held for too long. Care must be taken not to overstep your limits.

Candle Blowing Qi Training

The other Lian Qi exercise consists of blowing at a candle. This can be done profitably at any stage of your Qi Gong training.

Take a seat and place a lit candle about two feet on a table in front of you at the same level as your mouth. Press your tongue against your palate and purse your lips to form a small opening. Blow the air steadily through this orifice so as to bend the candle flame without extinguishing it. Use your abdominal muscles to do the blowing. You should continue for as long as possible without straining, making sure that your breath is uniform from beginning to end.

Gradually increase the distance between your lips and the candle flame until you can keep up a steady air flow at a distance of four feet or more.

> **The Benefits:** If you do this Lian Qi for five minutes every day, you will strengthen your abdominal muscles and increase pressure on the internal viscera.

> **Caution:** Overexertion in blowing can lead to dizziness.

Qi Gong masters recommend that Nei Dan breathing exercises be followed by a spot of massage and some loosening up exercises. It is argued that, in this way, any residual Qi in the body cavities will be removed. Stagnating Qi is said to obstruct normal Qi circulation and to cause discomfort.

SELF-MASSAGE

A professional massage might perhaps be the ideal way to rub down after a Nei Dan Qi Gong session. One may not be readily available, however. Therefore, Qi Gong tradition has evolved a series of easily learned techniques for self-massage.

The Head

Take a comfortable seat. Place the fingers of both hands against the scalp and rub the whole surface of the head by means of small circles. Then place your fingers along the center line of your scalp and move the whole scalp quickly backward and forward a dozen times. Move your fingers back along the scalp and repeat. End the massage when you have reached the back of your neck. At this point press your fingers against the top of your spine and rub firmly downward to the base of the neck.

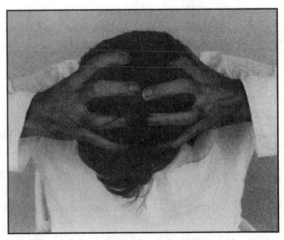

Figure 42: Head massage

The Benefits: This massage has the additional advantage of relieving headache. It also stimulates the hair roots and may prove effective against hair loss and gray hair.

Caution: None. But be sensible. Don't rub so vigorously as to pull the hairs out.

Ming Gu, Beating the Drum

Perhaps the most effective head massage known to Taoist monks is Ming Gu. It is generally used after deep breathing and meditation to clear the mind and flush away any stagnant Qi.

Tap vigorously on the top of your head with your fingertips.

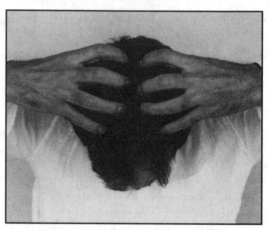

Figure 43: Ming Gu, beating the drum

The Benefits: It is said to improve memory and intelligence.

Caution: None.

The Face

Use the flat of the hand and the fingers to rub the brow and forehead.

Press with your thumbs against the bony rims of your eye sockets where they connect with the nose. Remove the pressure and slide your thumb about a third of an inch along the upper rim. Press again. Repeat until you have pressed around the entire rim of your eye sockets. Use your index finger instead of your thumb for the lower rim.

Massage from the bridge of the nose outward. Lightly massage your cheeks from below your eyes to your ears.

Press your philtrum firmly with your index finger (or thumb). The philtrum is the spot just below the nose where it meets the center of the upper lip. Finally, press your thumbs on your jaw bone just below your ears and pull down to your chin.

The Benefits: Face massages are particularly refreshing. Try it on your friends and family or even your pets. Get them to reciprocate. A face massage is even more relaxing when done by someone else.

This massage refreshes the brain, removes drowsiness, combats headaches, and tones up the muscles of the face.

Caution: Special care must be taken never to press too hard around the eyes in case the finger slips. This can be painful! Always rest your other fingers or your thumb on your forehead or cheek when massaging the eye rim. This ensures greater control of the thumb, or finger, doing the actual massage.

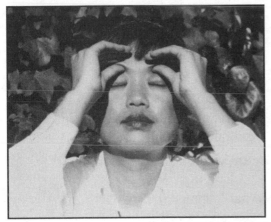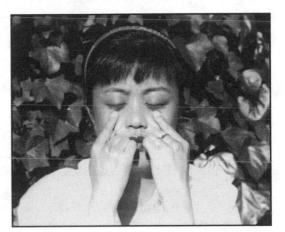

Figure 44 A & B: Face massage

The Teeth

Ke Chi, or teeth snapping, is normally used with the Ming Gu head massage after Nei Dan breathing exercises. Snap your teeth about thirty times. You will probably find that you are secreting more saliva than usual. At the end of the exercise, rinse your mouth with the saliva and swallow.

The Benefits: It is said to help protect against tooth decay.

Caution: Don't snap too hard as this can damage the teeth, especially if you have cavities.

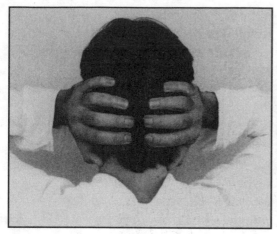
Figure 45: Ear massage

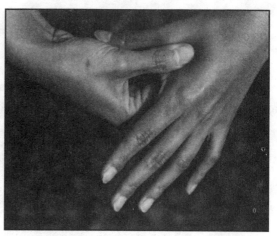
Figure 46: Hand massage

The Ears

Place the palms of your hands over your ears and tap on the back of the skull using your index and middle fingers. Repeat twenty to thirty times.

The Benefits: Refreshing, removes drowsiness and headaches.

Caution: Don't press the palms too hard against the ears.

The Hands

Rub your hands vigorously together then rub the center of each palm with the opposite thumb.

Pinch the cavity between your thumb and forefinger with the thumb and fingers of the other hand. The sensation is quite painful. Ignore the pain. Press and relax fifty times.

The Benefits: The exercise is supposed to cure toothaches, a sore throat, ear troubles, and neuralgia in the arms.

Caution: None; just make sure your nails are not cutting into the flesh.

The Lower Back

Strip to the waist. Close your hands into a fist. Rub with the top of your fists against the lumbar region of your back. Pressure should be exerted diagonally downward from the middle of the back, below the rib cage, to the waist.

The Benefits: Good for lumbago, lower back pain, and posture.

Caution: Best done in a warm environment.

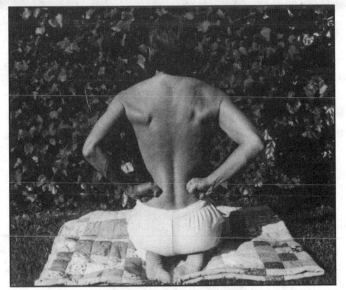

Figure 47: Lumbar massage

The Knees

Bare your knees:

1) Sit on a chair and press fairly hard on the tendon at the back of your bent knees. Repeat thirty times.
2) Hold your kneecaps with your fingers and gently massage the rims with small circular motions of the hand.

The Benefits: Eliminates fatigue and stiffness from the lower limbs.

Caution: None as long as you are gentle on the kneecap.

The Feet

Place your foot on your opposite knee. Press and rub into the center of the sole of each foot with your thumb. Rub rapidly against the sides of your feet with your fingers. The sole of the foot is said, in both China and India, to be the seat of multiple nerve endings as well as of particularly sensitive acupoints. Different areas of the foot are said to correspond to different organs and Qi channels. Pressure and massage on the areas will thus enhance the flow of Qi throughout the body.

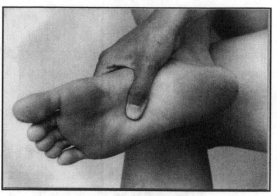

Figure 48

> **The Benefits:** Helps eliminate fatigue, helps digestion, and helps cure ailments of the stomach and the intestines. Pressure in the center of the sole stimulates circulation. Massage on the sides of the feet has shown to exert a beneficial effect on the organs of digestion and the spinal column.

> **Caution:** None.

LOOSENING UP EXERCISES

Most Qi Gong masters recommend several loosening up exercises after each session of Nei Dan breathing. Some advise one to perform the exercises prior to doing Nei Dan.

The recommended exercises consist of joint rotations and stretching. One is instructed, for example, to turn the head slowly from side to side, or to stretch the legs and back by grasping the feet. These movements closely resemble the asanas of Indian Hatha yoga. It is therefore the latter that are probably more appropriate for loosening up after Nei Dan breathing or, indeed, for preparing for it.

However, in order not to mix cultural traditions we should stick to Chinese exercises for Chinese Qi Gong. And that country has, in fact, developed an elaborate system of Wai Dan external techniques aimed specifically at getting the Qi circulating easily around the body.

Wai Dan Qi Gong can be practiced either before or after Nei Dan, or entirely independently from it.

Chapter Nine

—

Wai Dan Qi Gong

Wai Dan Qi Gong techniques are as important to Nei Dan Qi Gong as Hatha yoga postures are to Pranayama. Perhaps more so. During Nei Dan, Qi is made to circulate within the body but does not build up strength and suppleness in the muscles and the limbs. Wai Dan exercises aim to do this. The simplest Wai Dan exercises are intended to circulate and generate energy in all parts of the body thus ensuring health and longevity. Other, more complex Wai Dan systems aim further at transferring energy outside one's own body either for purposes of self defense or, purportedly, to cure other people's ailments. We shall not touch on these for two reasons. First, they involve many complicated movements which are not easy to learn from a text such as this. To try to do so would inevitably lead to mistakes in practice. Without guidance, a student cannot know if his or her posture, sequences, and speed are correct. Second, the martial arts have been practiced in the West for many years. Schools of Wu Shu, better known as Gong Fu (or Kung Fu) exist in most towns. There is little point therefore in going into a subject for which professional instruction abounds.

The Wai Dan exercises that follow are among the simplest. The first group is that taught by Bodhidharma when he emerged from his long meditation in Shaolin. It is from these basic movements that Shaolin Wu Shu and subsequently all forms of martial arts grew and evolved. The second group is called Ba Duan Jin, or Eight Pieces of Brocade, indicating, by its name, that there is beauty involved in the practice of the eight positions. Various versions of Ba Duan Jin have been popular in China since time immemorial. The version developed by General Yue Fei in the twelfth century and a Tang dynasty version attributed to Zhong Li are the two explored in this text. The last sequence described below is an extremely basic and simple form of Tai Ji Quan. Anything more complex cannot be taught in writing without errors becoming inevitable. By following the instructions carefully the following exercises can be practiced with ease.

DA MO WAI DAN

Da Mo Wai Dan is the other Chinese name for the Buddhist monk Bodhidharma, or Da Mo, who brought Chan meditation and Shaolin fitness drills to China in the sixth century A.D.

Bodhidharma developed his drills for the emaciated monks of the Shaolin monastery. They aim not only at improving health, but at building up muscular power.

Da Mo Wai Dan consists of twelve exercises. These should be performed in sequence. In this way, the energy built up in one exercise is carried forward to the next.

Energy is built up by relaxing a muscle during inhalation and tensing it during exhalation. Each exercise consists of at least twenty such breaths.

The full sequence of twelve exercises should take about fifteen minutes. Longer sittings would include as many as fifty breaths per exercise.

Throughout the Da Mo Wai Dan exercises you should stand straight with your feet parallel to one another about two feet apart.

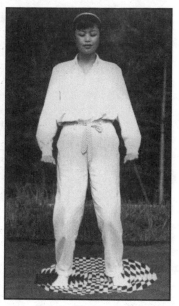

Figure 49: Exercise 1

Exercise 1

Stand with your feet apart as instructed above. Hold your arms by your sides with your elbows slightly bent and your palms open toward the ground. Your fingers should be pointing forward. Inhale slowly and uniformly. Exhale and imagine pressing firmly downward with your hands. In this exercise Qi is built up in the wrist.

Exercise 2

Maintain the same position as in Exercise 1. Close your hands into fists with your thumbs extended toward your body. During exhalation, imagine tightening your fists and pushing backward with your thumbs. In actual fact, your wrists should only be slightly tensed. This builds up energy in your hands and fingers.

Figure 50: Exercise 2

Da Mo Wai Dan

Figure 51: Exercise 3   *Figure 52: Exercise 4*   *Figure 53: Exercise 5*

Exercise 3

Maintain the same position. Close your thumb over your fingers into a normal fist. Turn your fists with the inside of your wrists toward your body. Inhale and imagine tightening your fists while exhaling. This builds up energy in the whole of the lower arm.

Exercise 4

Keep your fists clenched and extend your arms in front of you, the insides of your wrists facing inward. Imagine firmly clenching your fists during your exhalation. This drill will build up Qi energy in your chest and shoulders.

Exercise 5

Now raise your arms further until they are straight above your head. Maintain the fist position of your hands. Imagine clenching your fists while breathing out. In this exercise Qi is built up in the shoulders, neck, and the flanks.

Da Mo Wai Dan

Figure 54: Exercise 6   *Figure 55: Exercise 7*   *Figure 56: Exercise 8*

Exercise 6

Bend your elbows and lower your fists to within six inches of your ears. The insides of your wrists should be facing forward. Relax and slowly inhale. Clench your fists and exhale. As you breathe out, imagine pushing forward and upward with your fists. This builds up Qi in the flanks, upper torso, and arms.

Exercise 7

Keeping your fists clenched, extend your arms sideways, parallel to the ground. The insides of your wrists should be facing forward. Inhale. Exhale and tighten your fists. Feel the strength building up in your arms and chest. In this exercise, Qi is strengthened in the upper torso.

Exercise 8

Bring the extended arms forward, in front of you. Bend your elbows slightly giving a circular effect to the position of your arms. Inhale and relax. Clench your fists during the following exhalation. This builds up Qi in the arms and shoulders.

Da Mo Wai Dan

Figure 57: Exercise 9   *Figure 58: Exercise 10*   *Figure 59: Exercise 11*

Exercise 9

Pull your clenched fists back, from the previous position, toward your face. Bend your elbows and hold your fists, palms forward, just in front of your cheeks. Relax as you breathe in, then imagine tightening your fists and arm muscles during your exhalation. Qi is further enhanced in the arms and shoulders.

Exercise 10

Pull your elbows back and raise your forearms so that your fists are held about a foot from each side of your head. Clench your fists during your exhalations. This form is designed to start circulating the Qi accumulated in your shoulders.

Exercise 11

Keeping your elbows bent as in Exercise 10, lower your fists to a position immediately in front of your Dan Tian (about four inches below your navel). Imagine clenching your fists during your exhalations; mentally guide the Qi through your arms. In this exercise Qi is no longer accumulated but is now recovered.

Exercise 12

Unclench your fists, straighten your elbows, and raise your arms straight out in front of you. Hold your palms facing skyward. When exhaling imagine lifting a heavy weight with your arms. Inhale and relax. On your subsequent exhalation, raise your arms further until your palms are above the level of your head. Again, in this form, Qi is recovered for redistribution around the body.

When you have completed the whole Wai Dan sequence, it is advisable to sit or lie down in one of the Nei Dan Qi Gong positions (see chapter 10) in order to relax with a few minutes of normal breathing.

Figure 60: Exercise 12

The Benefits: General strengthening of the body, muscles, joints, and inner organs. These exercises improve circulation. They ensure the equilibrium of the nervous system as a whole. They build up resistance to disease.

Caution: None if practiced with moderate exertion. To start with do not exceed twenty breaths in each position, more than that at the beginning and you will feel fatigued and sore. With practice, you should build up to fifty inhalations and exhalations for each exercise.

BA DUAN JIN, THE EIGHT PIECES OF BROCADE

One of the most popular Wai Dan exercises derived directly from Bodhidharma's original sequence is the Song Dynasty's General Yue Fei's version of the Ba Duan Jin, or Eight Pieces of Brocade. General Yue Fei instituted these exercises for his troops' daily workouts in the twelfth century when he was successfully defending his country against the nomadic invasions from the northern steppes.

Ba Duan Jin is performed standing with back and head erect. In most of the eight forms, the feet are kept parallel about two feet apart. The exercises should be performed slowly so as to ensure that breathing is always calm and uniform. Always breathe through your nostrils.

The eight drills should be performed in sequence and each drill should be repeated three, four, or five times, depending on how long you wish to spend on the whole series.

Exercise 1: Head Turning

Stand erect with your feet apart. Inhale slowly and uniformly. Exhale and, during your exhalation, turn your head as far round as you can to your left. Look as far behind you as possible. Complete the movement and your exhalation together. Inhale and turn your head back to face the front. Repeat this sequence toward the right.

> **The Benefits:** Strengthens your neck muscles and those governing the movements of the eyes. It prevents problems from developing in the cervical vertebra. Blood circulation to the head is stimulated with resulting benefits to people suffering from hypertension and arteriosclerosis.

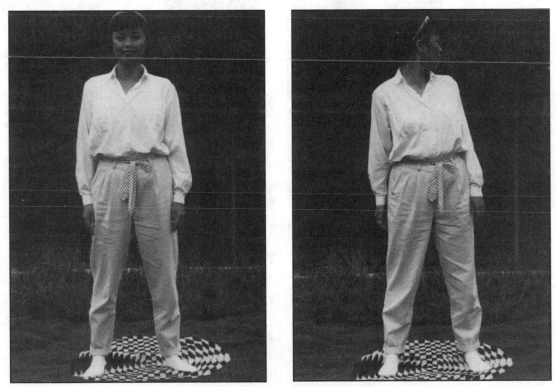

Figure 61 A & B: Ba Duan Jin, head turning 1

Exercise 2: Arm Stretching

Maintain your position. Interlock your fingers and hold your hands, palms down, in front of your abdomen. Inhale. While exhaling swing your arms slowly over your head, your palms facing skyward and stretch, standing on toes at the same time. Return to the starting position during your inhalation.

The Benefits: Relieves fatigue and strengthens the muscles of the back. It helps to correct bad posture.

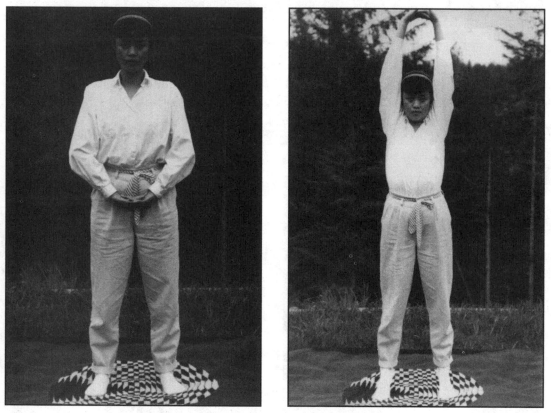

Figure 62 A & B: Ba Duan Jin arm stretching

Exercise 3: Single Arm Raising

Maintain your standing position. Hold your hands, palms up and fingers stretched out with the tips touching, in front of your navel. Inhale slowly. During your exhalation, move both arms simultaneously. Slowly raise your right hand over your head with your palm skyward and your fingers pointing to the left. Lower your left hand to below your waist, holding the palm downward and your fingers stretched forward. Inhale and return to your starting position. Repeat with the other hands.

The Benefits: Massages the internal organs of digestion thus preventing gastrointestinal problems.

Figure 63 A & B: Ba Duan Jin, single arm raising

Exercise 4: Drawing the Bow

Maintain your standing position and hold your clenched fists at your hips, your elbows bent behind you. Inhale and, with your left foot, take a short step to your left. Bend your knees a little and assume a horse riding stance. Exhale and turn your torso toward the left. At the same time bring your hands up in front of your left shoulder. Straighten the thumb and the index finger of your left hand. Rest your right fist on your left wrist. While still exhaling, keep your eyes on your outstretched left forefinger, extend your left arm away from you, parallel to the ground and, at the same time, draw your right fist across your chest to the right, as if pulling a bow. End the movement with your exhalation. Return to your starting position while inhaling. Repeat the exercise in the other direction.

The Benefits: This exercise strengthens the upper torso and the arms as well as improves circulation.

Figure 64 A, B & C: Drawing the bow

Exercise 5: Swaying the Head and Buttocks

Maintain the horse riding stance. Place your hands on your thighs with your fingers pointing inward. Inhale and shift the weight of your body forward onto your arms. Exhale and lean as far to your left as you can without losing your balance. End the movement with your exhalation. Return to your starting position as you inhale. Repeat toward the right.

The Benefits: It makes the spinal column more elastic and relaxes the nervous system.

Figure 65: Swaying the head and buttocks

Figure 66: Forward stretching

Exercise 6: Forward Stretching

Bring your feet closer together—between two feet apart to touching (the closer your feet, the more difficult the exercise). Stand straight and inhale. While exhaling bend forward to touch your toes with your fingers. Keep your legs as straight as possible. Do not bend them even if you can't reach your toes.

To begin with you may find that you can only keep your legs straight and touch your toes when your feet are apart. As you progress, try to bring your feet an inch closer together each day.

> **The Benefits:** Stretches the waist and the leg muscles thus improving their elasticity. It massages the abdominal viscera. Helps with sciatica problems.

> **Caution:** Lowering the head and thus flooding the higher regions with more blood should not to be attempted by people suffering from high blood pressure or arteriosclerosis. Always raise your head slowly afterward.

Exercise 7: Slow Punching

Adopt the horse riding stance. Inhale and hold your fists at your waist with your elbows bent behind you. Exhale and slowly punch up and to the right with your right fist. Keep your eyes on your fist throughout. Your arm should be straight and your fist level with the top of your head when you complete your exhalation. Return to your starting position during the following inhalation. Repeat with the left arm.

The Benefits: Stimulates the cerebral cortex and the nervous system, and promotes better circulation.

Figure 67: Slow punching

Exercise 8: Rising and Falling on the Toes

Stand to attention. Inhale. Raise your heels as high as possible during your exhalation. Lower your heels during the following inhalation.

The Benefits: Strengthens the lower legs and relaxes the rest of the body after the other seven exercises.

Caution: As for other exercises, never strain or overexert yourself in the beginning. A little soreness in the limbs is normal for the first few days of exercise. Fatigue, however, is not. Start with two repetitions of each drill and gradually work up to five or more when your body is used to it.

Figure 68: Heel raising

ZHONG LI'S BA DUAN JIN

Several versions of Ba Duan Jin have been developed over the centuries, many of these since the 1950s when interest was renewed in China for the ancient Qi Gong methods. There exists, however, one version of Ba Duan Jin that supersedes even General Yue Fei's development of Bodhidharma's Wai Dan. This was devised by Zhong Li during the Tang dynasty (618-907 A.D.).

Zhong Li's Ba Duan Jin version of the Eight Pieces Brocade is performed seated in one of the oriental cross-legged postures.

Exercise 1

Take your seat. Start by snapping your teeth together thirty-six times. The tip of your tongue should be pressed against your palate. Pause and breathe normally. Your mouth will have filled with saliva after the teeth snapping exercise. Rinse your mouth with the saliva and swallow it in three parts.

Place the palms of your hands over your ears with your fingers pointing backward. Tap the back of your head with your index and middle fingers twenty-four times.

Take a dozen deep and even breaths before moving on to the next form.

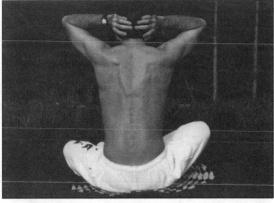

Figure 69

Exercise 2

Maintain your seat. Rest your left hand against your abdomen with the palm facing upward. Place your right palm in your left and close your fingers around the other hand. Exhale and turn your head as far to the left as you can. Turn back as you inhale. Do the same to the right repeat twenty-four times.

Figure 70

Figure 71 A & B

Exercise 3

Maintain your seat with your palms resting on your knees. Clench your fists and inhale slowly. Raise your arms above your head as you exhale. Maintain the position during the subsequent inhalation. Circle your tongue around your mouth to produce saliva. Swallow your saliva in three parts while imagining the Qi spreading from your heart to the rest of your body.

Exercise 4

Strip to the waist and rub your palms vigorously together in order to generate heat. Place your warm hands against your lower back and rub up and down thirty-six times. Return your hands to the resting position against your abdomen and breathe slowly and uniformly while imagining the Qi spreading from your heart toward the Dan Tian in your abdomen.

Figure 72

Exercise 5

Maintain your seated position. Place the palm of your left hand against your stomach and your right hand on your hip. Twist your upper torso by moving your left shoulder forward and your right one back. Repeat with your right shoulder forward. Keep your eyes straight ahead throughout. Inhale and exhale with each movement. Rotate your shoulders backward and forward thirty-six times.

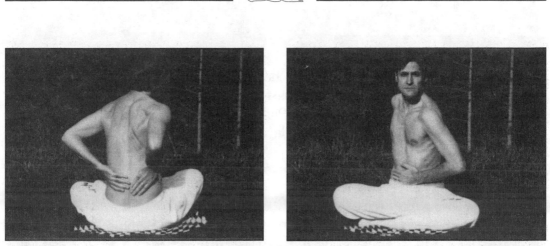

Figures 72 & 73

Exercise 6

Rub your palms together to generate warmth and place your hands over your kidneys as in Exercise 4. Push your shoulders back alternating first your left then your right. Repeat thirty-six times pushing your shoulders a little further back each time.

Rest your hands against your abdomen and breathe slowly and deeply. Imagine the heat of your Qi spreading from the Dan Tian through your lower abdomen, up your back and to the top of your head.

Exercise 7

Keep your seat and place your hands against your abdomen with your fingers interlocked and palms facing upward. Exhale and stretch your arms away from you and toward the sky. Point your palms away from your body throughout the exercise. As you inhale return your hands to the starting position against your abdomen. Repeat nine times.

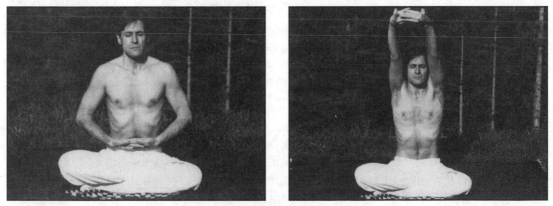

Figure 74 A & B

Exercise 8

Sit on the ground with your legs stretched out in front of you, your feet about two feet apart. Place the flat of your hands against the floor beside your thighs. Bend forward as you breathe out and grasp your toes. Pull on your feet and stretch you legs to the utmost. Inhale while returning to your starting position. Repeat the exercise twelve times.

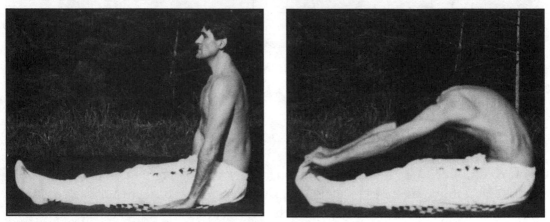

Figure 75 A & B

When you have completed one round of exercise, sit quietly for a few minutes with your eyes and mouth closed. Breathe slowly and evenly. Circle your tongue inside your mouth to produce saliva. Rinse your mouth with this and, once again, swallow in three parts. Before getting to your feet, shrug your shoulders and twist your torso.

> **The Benefits:** These exercises should tone up your whole system. You will probably find that you feel more relaxed, develop a sharper appetite, and sleep more soundly.

> **Caution:** None. The exercises are easy and gentle and can be performed by anybody.

TAI JI QUAN

We cannot adequately leave Qi Gong without some reference to the best known of all its forms: Tai Ji Quan, or, to use its more common westernized spelling, Tai Chi Chuan.

Although too intricate to learn without the guidance of an instructor, Tai Ji can be stripped down to a few essential movements. If practiced with attention to detail, these forms will provide you with a basic knowledge of what Tai Ji consists of.

Tai Ji means "the grand ultimate equilibrium" with reference to the Taoist theory of yin and yang. *Quan* means "boxing style." Tai Ji Quan is therefore obviously a Taoist martial art form which aims at the ultimate equilibrium of yin and yang. It is renowned for the slow elegance with which it is performed. Indeed, it probably resembles a slow oriental dance more than anything martial. During Tai Ji practice, the mind and body are relaxed. Attention is focused on developing a "swift waist" and on the Dan Tian. Qi is guided by the will, from the Dan Tian to different parts of the body. Strictly speaking, Tai Ji is therefore an internal, or Nei, form of Qi Gong.

Despite all this, Tai Ji forms are based on real combat situations and take names such as: push, pull, ward-off, shoulder-stroke, elbow-stroke, retreat, dodge, and advance. There are thirteen martial forms which include 128 movements in all. The following are among the simplest.

First Movement

Stand with your feet about eighteen inches apart.

Your toes should point slightly inward. Rest the weight of your body equally on the balls of both feet.

Your knees and shoulders should be straight and your back and neck erect. Draw in your abdomen slightly and concentrate on your Dan Tian, the internal energy point about three inches below your navel.

Bend your elbows and rest your hands against your abdomen, just below your ribs. Extend the fingers of both hands. The flat of your left hand should face upward, that of your right hand toward the ground. The palms of both hands should overlap. This hand position represents the equilibrium of yin (the left hand) and of yang (the right), which signifies perfect health.

Lower your eyelids, press the tip of your tongue against the roof of your mouth, and inhale slowly and evenly through your nostrils. Tai Ji is a Taoist exercise, so Fan Hu Xi, or "reverse breathing" is

Figure 76: Tai Ji Quan, first movement

used. Therefore contract your abdomen as you inhale. Feel the Qi in the air descending all the way to the Dan Tian. When you have finished inhaling, drop your tongue to its resting position and exhale through your mouth while expanding your abdomen.

Count fifteen such breaths before continuing with the second movement.

Tai Ji Quan

Figure 77: Second movement   *Figure 78: Third movement*   *Figure 79: Fourth movement*

Second Movement

Exhale and slowly extend both your arms in front of you. As you do so, turn the flat of your hands to face the front.

Your fingers should be joined and pointing skyward. Keep your arms parallel to the ground.

Breathe in evenly through your nostrils and contract your abdominal muscles. Hold the tip of your tongue against your palate. Relax your tongue as you exhale while expanding your abdomen.

Count ten breaths before proceeding.

Third Movement

On your last exhalation, swing your arms slowly outward so that they form a straight line with your shoulders. Keep your thumb and fingers pointing skyward. Continue breathing slowly and evenly through your nose. Count ten breaths.

Fourth Movement

Exhale and slowly swing your arms backward and up.

The flat of your hands should face the ground. Incline your body slightly forward and raise your arms as high as possible. Keep your arms pressed firmly against your upper rib cage. Maintaining the position, breathe slowly and evenly as before. Press your tongue against your palate and breathe through your nostrils. Count fifteen breaths.

These four movements should be performed in one continuous sequence lasting about five minutes. Having completed this basic series you may, if you wish, continue with another short sequence of three forms involving slightly more elaborate arm and foot movements.

First Form

Adopt the basic posture with head and neck erect and feet eighteen inches apart. Hold your hands against the top of your abdomen in the yin and yang "perfect health" position (see Movement 1).

Inhale through your nostrils and draw in your abdomen. During the exhalation, expand your abdomen and slowly turn your left hand level with your left shoulder while simultaneously turning your right hand away from you and level with your waist. The palms of both hands should face skyward as though you were carrying two bowls of water. Breathe slowly and evenly while making fifty slow circles with both hands.

Figure 80: Tai Ji Quan first form

Second Form

During your last exhalation, return your hands to their original position in front of your stomach, but do not adopt the "perfect health" pose. Hold your hands with the palms facing downward and the fingers extended. There should be at least three inches between the fingertips of the two hands. Pull your shoulders back and your elbows close to your body. Inhale.

While exhaling, bend your knees as if you were about to take a seat. Slowly turn the palms of your hands toward one another. Tense your fingers. Inhale, then slowly extend your arms and straighten your body as you exhale. Inhale and return to your starting position. Repeat this movement between thirty and fifty times.

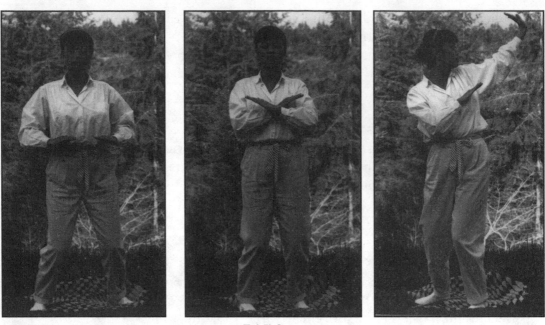

Tai Ji Quan

Figure 81: Second form   **Figure 82 A & B: Tai Ji Quan third form**

Third Form

Maintaining the center of gravity in your lower abdomen, lift your left foot and bring it to within nine inches of the other. Cross your wrists in front of your chest. Keep your fingers loosely extended and the flat of your hands facing the ground. As you exhale, slowly swing your left arm away from your body, turn the palm skyward. Keep your elbow slightly bent. Turn your waist, shoulders, and head together as you do this. Inhale, then with the next exhalation, swing back and continue the movement until your right arm is extended slightly away from the body. Slowly swing back and forth about fifty times.

Guidelines have been given as to when to breathe in and out during the above forms. However, you should ignore these altogether to start with. Breathe normally, in your own time, as you get to grips with the basic movements. If you wish to develop Tai Ji further, you will later be able to apply the principles of Taoist abdominal breathing to your movements.

The Benefits: Tai Ji tones up the digestive, nervous, and respiratory systems. It is also an effective remedy for heart, circulation, and pulmonary disorders, as well as for rheumatism and arthritis.

Caution: None. The initial side effects may include a slight ache in the limbs if you haven't exercised much before. You might also experience shivers in your arms. These should disappear after a few weeks of practice but may be replaced by other reactions such as gastric and intestinal gasses, greater perspiration, hiccups, and increased secretion of saliva. All of these are frequent side effects of the practice of Tai Ji and are therefore nothing to worry about.

After six months of steady practice, you should begin to feel extremely relaxed and comfortable every time you sit down to your Qi Gong sessions, so much so, in fact, that you may begin to feel edgy if you have to miss a sitting.

The Wai Dan exercise forms that have been illustrated above are only the simplest ones. As one progresses with Tai Ji Quan, many, more complex movements of attack and defense are developed.

Chapter Ten

—

Qi Gong in a Hurry

The ideal daily practice of Qi Gong will include Nei Dan internal circulation of Qi followed by massage and a session of Wai Dan exercises. Not everyone, however, can afford to spend so much time, every day, circulating the Qi. Some easier, less time-consuming Qi Gong practices are therefore worth exploring.

The following ten-minute Qi Gong breaks can be practiced standing, sitting, lying in bed, or on a walk.

To begin with you might need a quiet environment to aid your concentration. Later, however, you should be able to practice anywhere: at the bus stop, in your car, in a plane, or at the office.

The Standing Position

This is the position already described in chapter 8 (page 92).

Stand with your feet shoulder-width apart. Your toes should be pointing slightly inward. Bend your knees. Feel the weight of your body on your calf muscles and balls of your feet, not on your thighs or heels. (The Chinese say *imagine that there are ants running around under your heels. Make sure that you do not put so much weight on your heels or you will squash them.*) You can adjust the intensity of the exercise by varying the degree at which your knees are bent.

Your head and back should be erect, your arms raised in front of you with elbows bent, and hands level with your shoulders. Your arms must be rounded as if encircling a large balloon. Keep your shoulders lowered and your fingers slightly splayed.

To begin with you should adopt this position for ten minutes and breathe normally. Later you can combine the breathing with an imaginary movement of your arms.

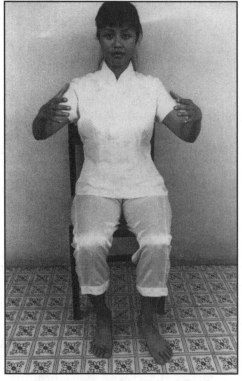

Imagine holding a large elastic rubber ball in your arms. Press inward on the ball as you breathe in. Feel the resistance against your hands and arms. Relax as you breathe out. You may, if you wish, enhance the effect by actually moving your arms in and out slightly with your breathing.

> **The Benefits:** This is Qi Gong's most important pose. It strengthens the muscles of the back, legs, arms, and abdomen as well as ensuring all the benefits of Qi circulation to the muscles, joints, internal organs, and nervous system. See chapter 2 for the benefits of Qi Gong.

> **Caution:** Do not overexert yourself in the beginning. The position looks easy but, because of the unusual angle of the legs, a good deal of strain is put on the thighs as well as on the arms. Ten minutes of this position can lead to fatigue. Increase your time in the position gradually.

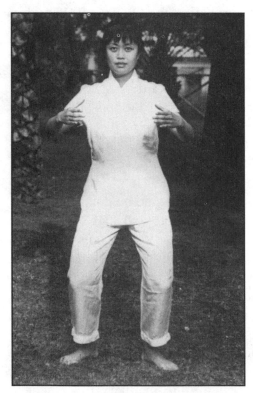

Figure 83: Qi Gong standing position

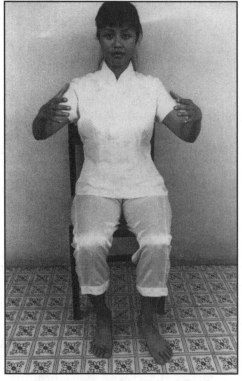

Figure 84: Qi Gong sitting position

The Sitting Position

This position differs from the one described previously in that all the Qi is concentrated in the upper half of the body.

You should be seated on a chair with your feet on the ground and with your trunk and head erect. Raise your arms as described for the standing position. The intensity of this exercise can be varied by adjusting the position of your arms. The further outstretched your arms, the more strenuous will be the exercise.

As in the standing position, breathe deeply and slowly while imagining the expansion and contraction of a balloon held in your arms.

> **The Benefits:** The same as those for the standing position except that the legs are not exercised.

> **Caution:** None, except that you may feel some soreness in your arms for the first few days.

The Lying Position

You should adopt the same arm position as in the two previous exercises while lying flat on your back. The wider apart you hold your hands, the more strenuous the exercise becomes.

Figure 85: Qi Gong lying position

> **The Benefits:** Practicing deep breathing in the lying position is a particularly effective remedy against insomnia. It is also an aid for lazy risers. Doing a stint of deep breathing with your arms

held out after the alarm rings can help gather your energies for getting up and about.

Apart from sleeping problems, the exercise is best for convalescents, the very old or the very weak. It allows the Qi to circulate within the body, thus strengthening the nervous system and the inner organs, without putting any strain on the muscles and joints.

Caution: None.

Xing Bu Gong, or Walking Control

This exercise combines Qi Gong breathing with walking.

Stand straight with your hands by your side.

Breathe in and take a slow, gentle pace forward with your left foot. The outside of your heel should touch the ground first. Roll the ridge of your foot on the ground until your toes hold the weight of your body and your heel is slightly raised. Now bring your right foot forward for the second pace, again placing your heel, ridge of your foot, and toes on the ground in that order. Walk in this way for two hundred paces.

Your arm and hand movement should accompany your paces as follows: As your left leg swings forward, stretch your arms diagonally from your chest out toward the left. Your hands should be at shoulder level with your left palm upward and your right facing left. Bend your elbows in order to pull your arms back and, in

Figure 86: Xing Bu Gong, walking control

one continuous motion, stretch out toward the right as you bring your right foot forward. Alternate in this manner with each pace you take.

Coordinate your breathing with your paces by breathing in when you take a left step and out with your right step.

> **The Benefits:** Xing Bu Gong is an effective therapy for some chronic conditions such as diabetes and obesity.

> **Caution:** It may be performed either slowly or at a brisk pace, according to personal preference. Do not worry if you cannot coordinate your breathing and your walking very easily at first. Just walk, swing your arms, and think about the breathing afterward.

Chapter Eleven

—

Breathing and Sexuality

Oriental breathing techniques' principal concern is the healthy circulation of vital energy—Qi, or Prana. There is no greater energy-generating human activity than sex.

During the sex act breath rhythms change, the heart beats faster, and partners share and exchange their energy in a million different ways—from a gentle caress to life-giving seed. The ancient Taoists knew this when they practiced ritual sex for the enhancement of their Qi. The Hindu and the Buddhist Tantrics knew it when they called down the male and female forces of the cosmos into their lovemaking. As a consequence, they studied the interplay between sex, energy, and breathing, and handed down their methods and findings to subsequent generations of adepts.

We have already mentioned how Tantric yogis believed that by harmonizing the left, lunar, and feminine breath with the right, solar, and masculine one, they would recreate within themselves the equilibrium of the universe. If this was done during sexual intercourse, they would assure themselves transcendence and liberation. Although there is intrinsically no reason why the following techniques may not be practiced by lovers of the same sex, it should be pointed out that both Tantrism and Taoism do not envisage homosexual sex at all. The reason is simple. Taoism and Tantrism are concerned with the exchange of male and female (yang and yin) energies. If the sex of the lovers is the same, the energies are the same thus rendering the entire exercise futile.

During Tantric lovemaking the left and right breaths are harmonized both within themselves and with each other. Partners lie on their sides facing one another and actively mix their inhalations and expirations. It has been observed by the Tantrics that lying on one side automatically causes the upper side nostril to become dominant: if one lies on one's left flank, the right nostril is dominant.

133

The man should thus lie on his left side facing his partner. He should exhale through his right nostril and she should inhale the same air through her left nostril, and vice versa. The resulting ecstasy is supposed to bind their souls together in eternal love.

As a spin-off to this technique, the left or right nostril dominance is said to affect the sex of any child conceived at that moment. Right nostril dominance in the man and left dominance in the woman at the moment of ejaculation should assure a male heir. If it is the other way round, the child should be a girl. If, however, one gets it wrong and the same side is dominant in both partners the resulting offspring might well be homosexual.

In Taoist sex, the circulation of Qi is paramount. Nei Dan circulation can be extended to one's partner at all levels of intimacy. Lovers can circulate their Qi independently and then share their energy through mutual massage or merely lying in one another's arms. One technique begins with both lovers lying naked next to each other, each engaged in Xiao or Da Zhou Tian (Small or Grand Circulation) abdominal breathing. One partner should then stand, or kneel beside or even straddle the other's body and touch the center of his (or her) partner's forehead with extended fingertips. He (let us imagine that the man is the active partner) should then run the flat of his hand gently over his partner's body to the Dan Tian area of the abdomen. He should try to synchronize his movement with her inspiration. He can caress her body and her limbs in this way while she continues with her Da Zhou Tian Grand Circulation exercise. No words should be spoken throughout, all communication being only physical.

Afterward, each partner can massage the other according to Qi Gong massage techniques.

During lovemaking itself, partners can enhance the natural Qi exchanges of love simply by continuing to practice Xiao Zhou Tian or Da Zhou Tian Nei Dan. The lovers may either lie next to one another or adopt one of the oriental cross-legged positions. In the latter case, the man should hold his lover on his lap, drawing her body close to his own while she crosses her legs behind his back. Initially, the movements of love should be imperceptible as each partner meditates on the inner flow of Qi. Sexual arousal to the point of orgasm is not important here. It is the quiet convergence and exchange of Qi that the lovers should be aiming for, not the release of passion.

The concept that orgasm is best avoided reappears in Tantric traditions. According to Tantric physiology, the Kundalini serpent must rise from the bottom of the spine, through the seven chakras, or energy centers, in order to pierce the thousand petaled lotus at the top of the head and thus bring enlightenment. Any dispersal of energy through orgasm will block the Kundalini at the second chakra, behind the genitals. Tantric love therefore aims at a static embrace through which female energy, Sakta, is absorbed by the male partner.

Sometimes, however, sexual passion may get the best of a person and ejaculation become inevitable. As long as this happens only two or three times in ten, there is said to be no serious dispersion of energy. If it happens more often, Tantric practice comes to the rescue with kumbhaka and bandhas. The following passage is from the Buddhist *Chandamaharosana Tantra.*

> *He should retain his breath and contract the lower stomach. Visualizing the Divine Buddha Chandamaharosana in sexual union with the Goddess of Wisdom and energy, he should press his heel against the base [the perineum] and his tongue against the roof of his mouth. By concentrating his wavering thoughts and controlling his breath, the adept will prevent his semen from moving outward.* [1]

The Taoists advise similar techniques involving breath retention, psychological distractions, and physical pressure on various acupoints. Better still, though, is the regulation of breathing throughout the act of love. If a man maintains a steady abdominal respiration through his nostrils and refrains from gasping or panting, he should be able to accomplish at least five thousand love strokes before ejaculating. At an average rate of one stroke per second that would amount to one hour, twenty-three minutes solid of love making.

The best of luck to anyone who wants to try.

For this sort of lovemaking to be mutually satisfying it is indispensable that both partners be physically fit enough to go the full distance. Once again, regular practice of Qi Gong, Pranayama, and yoga can make the difference between a tired, unconvincing performance and one that transports to the heights of sexual bliss.

Well-exercised lungs and muscles ensure greater staying power in the man. The woman too can benefit from stronger back and leg muscles. The increased strength from exercise can help her lift her pelvis higher during frontal sex thus increasing stimulation of the clitoris and easier orgasm. The female orgasm also involves an increase in the flow of blood to the genitals. The better the circulation, the easier and better will be the orgasm. Breathing exercises that improve circulation will therefore improve orgasm as well.

Finally, there are psychosexual benefits to be derived from practice of Pranayama, yoga, and Qi Gong. Relaxing deep breathing after the distracting activities of the working day can prepare one for enhanced sexual pleasure. Love after a stint of Qi Gong or Pranayama is usually a subtler, gentler experience than after dinner, TV, or even oysters and champagne. There is, indeed, no greater aphrodisiac than the mellow, tender mood that comes upon one after gentle breathing exercises.

All Pranayama and Nei Dan Qi Gong techniques performed in one of the seated positions enhance the mood for love. A few minutes of relaxation after the breathing is even better.

The specific yoga postures that tone up the sexual organs of the body are: Halasana (the Plow), Bhujangasana (the Cobra), Ardha-Matsyendrasana (the Spinal Twist), and Yoga Mudra (the symbol of yoga). See chapter 7 for details of these asanas.

....

....

....

Chapter Twelve

—

Health Conditions

"Western medicine cures the disease,
Oriental techniques cure the patient."[1]

A person's health depends on both external and internal factors. Poor hygiene, pollution, and haphazard viral infections are responsible for the kinds of disease that find their way into the human organism from the outside. The way that an organism reacts depends on heredity, diet, degree of stress in one's lifestyle, and physical fitness.

Some of these factors, like heredity and pollution, are beyond one's control. Others, notably diet, hygiene, stress, and fitness are, however, wholly within the individual's power to influence. Among these, stress and physical fitness are directly affected by the practice of Pranayama or Qi Gong.

Pranayama and Qi Gong prevent the onset of disease by building up the body's resistance to it. They massage the internal organs, increase oxygen intake, and tone up the nervous system. Regular practice therefore increases one's chances of maintaining good and long-lasting health.

Unfortunately, most people tend to forget about their health while they have it. They eat poorly, are too lazy to exercise, and live in a condition of near permanent tension, swallowing a few pills whenever anything goes wrong. It is only when the pills fail to work that people start worrying, and turn elsewhere for a cure to their ailments. Then, perhaps even Pranayama and Qi Gong might be taken seriously as a measure of last resort.

In China, the popularity of Qi Gong is such that one comes across many weird and wonderful stories about Qi Gong therapy that are nothing short of miraculous.

People are cured of cancer in a month, Qi Gong masters lay on hands and their patients are at once cured of the deadliest diseases. Some even purport to heal at a distance, by mind power alone.

Most of these tales are of course just that—only tales. Few of them are corroborated by any serious scientific evidence. Nevertheless, despite the lack of scientific corroboration or, indeed, of a theory to describe the phenomenon, one does come across seemingly genuine personal case histories that appear to offer evidence of healing through the practice of therapeutic Qi Gong.

Since the foundation of the Beijing Qi Gong Institute in 1979, numerous Qi Gong training centers have been set up in workplaces and in parks all over China. Hundreds of instructors teach Qi Gong therapeutic exercises to many thousands of patients in Beijing alone. It is from the personal experiences of these patients that the case histories quoted in this chapter were taken.[2]

According to a study published by the Institute, about 25 percent of the patients who practice Qi Gong assiduously for three years or more, are completely cured of their ailments. Another 45 percent experience remarkable improvement without, however, achieving a permanent cure. Twenty percent benefit only marginally while the remaining 10 percent make no progress at all.

The later a person resorts to Pranayama and Qi Gong, the less effective these exercises will be. Nevertheless, some good they can always do both in strengthening the body as a whole and in combating specific disorders.

It is important to start exercising gently, particularly if you are weak or convalescing. You should never exert yourself when the illness is at its worst. It is probably advisable, in these circumstances, to lie down and practice only the mildest deep breathing techniques three or four times a day.

Bearing the above points in mind, we can now consider which Pranayama and Qi Gong techniques are most suited to different ailments. All the recommended exercises are of scientifically proven benefit to patients attending yoga therapy centers in India[3] as well as to those practicing Qi Gong in China's modern Qi Gong institutes and centers. They cannot, of course, be regarded as alternatives to professional medical help, but only as a support to a complete course of treatment. If you suffer from one of these health conditions, please consult your doctor before embarking on an exercise routine.

Finally, to quote Svatmarama:

> *In all diseases the skillful physician should carefully administer treatment according to the methods described by the science of medicine and also administer yogic treatment.*[4]

AGING

Until a few years ago it was generally believed that aging was beyond human control. The fact that some people looked younger, and behaved more youthfully than others was attributed to genes, luck, and plastic surgery. Recent research has, however, shown that, although genes and luck are involved, the way a person lives has a direct bearing on the aging process.

As a person grows older, the body does not assimilate nutrients as efficiently as it did in youth, toxins and poisons build up, and free radicals gradually attach to and damage living cells. By increasing one's consumption of the essential nutrients, flushing out toxins, and minimizing the effects of free radicals you can, in effect, actively slow down the processes of aging.

A high-fiber diet of fresh, raw vegetables, fruits, grains, seeds, and nuts with proteins from soy products and fish will generally provide the necessary nutrients. Vitamin and enzyme supplements can also help. It is recommended that one eats less as one grows older. The body needs more essential nutrients but less bulk and protein as it ages. It seems likely, from experiments with rats, that by drastically reducing the intake of calories an individual can live 50 percent longer. It has yet to be proven that this works with humans although it is reasonable to assume that if a person puts less strain on the digestive system and, at the same time, increases the quality of nutrients, his or her body will stay healthier longer.

A person should avoid alcohol, sugar, fat, caffeine, drugs, chemicals, and pollutants whenever possible, and drink plenty of pure water and natural fruit juices.

To flush toxins out of the system regular fasting seems to be the answer (see page 32).

To lessen the damaging effect of free radicals two strategies are available: Minimizing their development within the body and destroying them by ingesting free radical scavengers. Free radicals are atoms with at least one unpaired electron. Unpaired electrons combine with other elements in the body to cause damaging chemical reactions. They can, for example, alter the structure of genetic coding in proteins, which can lead to cancer, or they can destroy the protective film of fat surrounding cells and bring about unhealthy fluid retention within these cells —the cause of aging.

Free radicals come into being through the ordinary metabolic process of oxidation. When one eats, and when one exercises, the body uses oxygen to create energy. In the process, unstable oxygen free radicals are released. These attach themselves to, and damage, living cells. Small quantities of oxygen free radicals are kept in check by the normal processes in the body. However, when the body ages or when external events bring about the formation of massive doses of free radicals, natural defenses cannot cope. In these circumstances, the ingestion of antioxidants vitamins C and E, beta-carotene, and selenium will seek out and destroy free radicals within the body.

However, eliminating the causes of free radical release is probably a more reasonable strategy whenever possible. Free radical activity is intensified by a diet high in fats—especially fried fats—and by strenuous exercise. Eliminating fried foods from your diet is fairly easy. Eliminating strenuous exercise, on the other hand, would appear to go against the entire theory of the beneficial effects of physical fitness. Note, however, that we have specified that strenuous exercise intensifies the formation of free radicals, not reasonable fitness programs based on walking, swimming, yoga, or Qi Gong.

Indeed, few athletes maintain their build and efficiency far into middle age—muscles turn to fat and free radicals cause havoc to the bodily structures. Yoga and Qi Gong masters, on the other hand, remain fit, energetic, and supple to the very end of their lives. Swami Krishna, of the Divine Life Society in Rishikesh, U.P., India, dedicated his whole life to the practice of Hatha yoga exercises. When I studied with him in 1977, his facial wrinkles, baked by seventy or more years in the Indian sunshine, showed his true age; his body, however, was that of a fit, twenty-five-year-old athlete. Master Hai Deng of Shaolin Monastery in Henan Province, China, was able, when in his nineties, to perform a vertical handstand on two fingers; his beard was gray but his body was as fit as that of a healthy man in his forties.

Any full and regular program of Pranayama and yoga or Nei Dan and Wai Dan Qi Gong will maintain the body fit and supple without the damaging effect of free radical release. Deep breathing with thirty second kumbhaka breath retention in particular will improve blood and tissue oxygenation and combat the formation of free radicals.

AIDS (ACQUIRED IMMUNE DEFICIENCY SYNDROME)

Over ten years into the AIDS epidemic it is becoming apparent that some HIV carriers are able to stave off the onset of full-blown AIDS indefinitely. As for most illnesses, a good deal probably depends on luck—on good genes and freedom from infective agents. However, it would appear that, for many HIV carriers, building up the immune system is the one single factor that has so far kept AIDS at bay. A healthy diet, appropriate supplements, a positive psychological outlook, and a suitable exercise program seem to be the factors that ensure a well functioning immune system.

A healthy diet of mostly raw, nutritious food with adequate supplements of vitamins is essential (see chapter 3, page 29). So is the practice of regular twenty-four- or thirty-six-hour fasts which flush pollutants and toxins from the body. It is also obvious that one should refrain, as far as possible, from putting toxins into the body in the first place. Alcohol, drugs, and tobacco are therefore anathema to anyone HIV positive hoping to stave off AIDS.

An optimistic outlook and suitable exercise program are both assured by the regular practice of Qi Gong, Pranayama, and Hatha yoga. Apart from toning up the body both inside and outside, the very discipline entailed in getting down to one's daily stint helps to cultivate the kind of positive mental attitude that can enhance all bodily functions including that of the immune system. In particular, deep breathing and relaxation have been shown, in the laboratory, to combat the effects of stress and to increase resistance to pathogens.

ALCOHOLISM

Small doses of alcohol have a dilatory and cholesterol cleansing effect on the arteries and veins. Or so it is suggested by both the two-time Nobel Prize-winner Linus Pauling (who advocates a shot of vodka a day) and by recent evidence (January 1993) that one glass of either red or white wine decreases the risk of clogged arteries and thus of heart attack. Larger doses, however, constitute a poison.

Regular consumption of alcohol causes metabolic damage to every cell in the body bringing about rapid aging, increasing susceptibility to disease and generally shortening one's life span by several years. Alcohol is broken down in the liver where it is converted into fat while, at the same time, destroying the cells of the liver itself. A damaged liver impairs the metabolism and the processes of digestion and absorption of proteins and vitamins. In short, dependency on alcohol, be it physical or psychological, will kill.

Weaning oneself off this poison is a question of will, first and foremost.

One drinks, perhaps, for social reasons, to change one's mood, to fight depression, or to celebrate. Later one drinks simply because one craves it.

Whatever the reason, if a person wants to rid him- or herself of the habit, than the person can. First of all, it is indispensable to make up one's mind to stay away from alcohol altogether—even one sip can bring about a relapse. Once the mind is made up, certain purifying techniques and exercises can be brought in to help.

It helps to change old environments and habits, to stay away from old drinking acquaintances, to meet people and make new friends not associated with the bad old drinking days. One can go out more; go for walks, go cycling, or travel. Changes to one's diet should be made in order to include more fresh fruit and vegetables, whole grains, nuts, and beans and less meat and fat. Fried and junk food are best avoided as are other unnecessary toxins such as drugs, tranquilizers, or tobacco. (For more about diet see chapter 3, page 29). A ten-day fast will help to detoxify the whole body (see page 32). Above all, regular deep breathing exercises to improve metabolism and oxygenate the blood and cells will help break the clutch of alcohol for good.

The specific exercises to practice are: Kapalabhati (see page 53) or Bhastrika (see page 55) followed by Ujjayi Pranayama (see page 58) and a fifteen-minute sequence of asanas: Halasana (the Plow), Dhanur (the Bow), and Ardha-Matsyendra (the Spinal Twist). One should always end with at least five minutes of relaxation in either a seated or lying (Shavasana) pose. This will help to focus the will and to calm the nerves—both necessary activities when the psyche is still fighting the body's compulsive cravings for alcohol. Wai Dan followed by Nei Dan Qi Gong will achieve similar results. Regular practice of Xing Bu Gong, or walking control (see page 130), is also considered useful.

ALLERGIES

An allergy is an inappropriate reaction of the body's defense mechanisms to a substance which, although not harmful, is treated as if it were. The immune system overreacts to the foreign substance by attacking it with white blood cells thus bringing about a series of symptoms, such as sneezing, asthma, or skin rash or, in some severe cases, anaphylactic shock—all of which cause more harm to the body than the foreign substance it is attacking.

Any substance in the world can bring about an allergy to somebody somewhere. The most common allergens (that is, substances which cause allergies) are: pollen, animal dander, molds, lanolin, some metals (especially nickel), insect bites and stings, some foods (strawberries and oysters for example), some chemical additives, such as MSG and sulfates, as well as some common medicines like aspirin and penicillin.

The underlying cause of allergic reactions to certain substances is unknown. There is evidence of certain allergies running in families as well as of the fact that babies who have not been breast-fed appear to suffer from them more than others. The only manageable factor that appears to have some bearing on allergies is stress. The more stressed one is, the more easily one appears to succumb to one's allergies.

This being the case, the obvious strategy in dealing with allergies is, first, to identify the allergen; secondly, to keep away from it, or them, as best one can; and third, to actively follow a healthy lifestyle and diet, and diminish stress.

Identifying the allergen may be more easily said than done. If you catch a cold every time you are in the presence of a cat, naming the culprit is easy. If, however, you come out with skin rashes quite frequently but do not know why, it might be an idea to put yourself through a food allergy self-test. First of all, keep a written record of everything you eat and refer to it whenever the skin rash reappears. When you have narrowed your search down to a few suspicious foods, try taking each of these foods in turn on an empty stomach. You will be able to identify the allergen if you measure your pulse rate immediately before and twenty minutes after eating. Be sure to be seated and relaxed when taking these measurements. If your pulse rate increases by more than ten pulsations per minute after ingesting the food, you have probably identified the allergen. Stay away from it and test again a few weeks later.

As well as the allergen, one should also eliminate as many unnecessary toxins as possible from the diet by cutting down, or dispensing altogether with coffee, alcohol, strong tea, cigarettes, and tobacco.

A diet should be healthy, and include plenty of greens, fruits, beans, and cereals with less meat and fats. A person should avoid hot and spicy foods, eat regular meals, never overindulge, and get up from the dinner table knowing that he or she could eat a little more. Dinner should be eaten at least three hours before bedtime, slowly, with food chewed properly. A person should also drink plenty of water, and, finally, cut down on stress by means of regular Qi Gong or Pranayama and yoga practice.

The specific exercises to combat stress are Nei Dan Qi Gong or Shavasana after a complete exercise program of Wai Dan Qi Gong or Hatha yoga respectively.

ANEMIA

Anemia involves a reduction of red blood cells and, as a consequence, in the amount of oxygen that the blood is able to carry. Its early symptoms are poor appetite, constipation, irritability, and headaches. Anemia is characterized by general fatigue and debility and by pallid nails and inner eyelids.

More than an illness in its own right, anemia is usually a symptom of some underlying problem. Some of the possible causes of anemia are poor diet, drug use, loss of blood from wounds, menstruation, an ulcer, a damaged liver, a thyroid disorder, or rheumatoid arthritis. Whenever anemia is suspected, a professional consultation to discover the underlying cause is thus mandatory.

Temporary, non-pathological anemia can be cured quite easily by increasing the intake of iron. Iron makes hemoglobin which carries oxygen in the blood. Good sources of iron are blackstrap molasses and, of course, iron tablets. Liver, or raw liver extract, contains the elements essential for reconstituting the red blood cells.

The usefulness of Pranayama and Qi Gong breathing exercises in cases of anemia is simply in ensuring a more efficient use of oxygen by the lungs and consequently an increased oxygenation of the blood. Pranayama with kumbhaka breath retention works best.

ANXIETY AND INSTABILITY

Short of resorting to the help of psychoanalysis, therapy, or counseling, yoga, Pranayama, and Qi Gong are, without doubt, the best remedies a person of an anxious or nervous disposition can turn to for help. They provide an ideal combination of physical exertion, control over the emotions, and introspection which lead to lasting calm and stability. The only real problem for a person of this disposition is getting down to a remedial program of Pranayama or Qi Gong in the first place, and then keeping at it. Emphasis on regularity and perseverance is thus paramount.

The following program is aimed specifically at calming and fortifying the nervous system as a whole:

Thirty rounds of Bhastrika, twenty rounds of Ujjayi Pranayama, followed by the following asanas to be repeated three times each:

- Uttanpadasana leg raising
- Halasana (the Plow)
- Bhujangasana (the Cobra)
- Sarvangasana (the Candle Stand)
- Matsyasana (the Fish)
- Dhanurasana (the Bow)
- Paschimottanasana forward stretch
- Chakrasana (the Wheel)
- Shirshasana head stand
- Shavasana relaxation or meditation for fifteen to twenty minutes

Please refer to chapter 7 for a full description of these asanas.

If the full sequence is considered too time consuming, Dhanur, Paschimottan, Chakra, and Shirsh asanas may be dispensed with.

A Qi Gong program serving the same purpose should start with ten to fifteen minutes of Nei Dan Circulation followed by self-massage, Tai Ji Quan, and, finally, fifteen minutes of relaxation.

Wang Lian Yi, forty years old when he started practicing Qi Gong in 1982, is a tourist guide and interpreter working for the National Tourism Bureau in

Beijing, who was suffering from an unspecified disorder of the autonomic nervous system.

At the beginning of 1980, Wang Lian Yi was sent abroad to interpret for a Chinese delegation. For three months his time was taken up entirely by a continuous round of meetings, conferences, and discussions. During this period, he slept no more than four hours per night. Finally, in April, exhaustion got the better of him and he fell prey to fits of dizziness, vomiting, and fainting. He was sent back to Beijing immediately.

In Beijing, he was diagnosed by the best specialists as suffering from a disorder of the autonomic nervous system. He spent the next two years in the hospital where he was given both Chinese and Western treatments. This resulted in only marginal improvement to his health.

In 1981, while still in hospital, Wang Lian Yi underwent massage and acupuncture treatment, but to no avail.

At the beginning of 1982 he returned to work, although he still suffered from nervous tension, dizziness, and irritability. He seemed unable to sit down to more than fifteen minutes of work at the time. As a consequence, he was generally low-spirited.

It was at work that a colleague suggested Qi Gong to him, but Wang was skeptical. "Then another colleague told me magic facts about the curative effects of Qi Gong," Wang Lian Yi recounts.

"He suggested that I should go to the Worker's Cultural Palace Park in Beijing where a Qi Gong training course was held every morning. I was still full of doubts. Nevertheless, in February I started going there every morning to watch. I talked to many patients who told me about their Qi Gong experiences and how their various ailments had been cured by it. I listened to the coach explain that far from being some farfetched magical essence, Qi was a material substance and that the practice of therapeutic Qi Gong had a scientific base. So I made up my mind to give it a try. On April, 7, 1982, I enrolled in the class.

"I took it very seriously, practicing two or three times a day. After twenty days, I started to feel Qi accumulating in my hands. This strengthened my resolve to continue. On May 15, according to my coach's instructions, I practiced Nei Dan Qi circulation in the standing position for the first time. I was at home, alone. During the exercise, I suddenly felt my body moving of its own accord. Although my mind was quite clear, my arms and trunk started moving in spontaneous Qi Gong patterns. The phenomenon lasted no more than thirty minutes, leaving me sweating but feeling comfortable.

"When I opened my eyes, I felt light-hearted and lucid. I felt as if I had emerged into a new world. The old feelings of dizziness had disappeared. I felt light and stable in my movements. I found that I could sit for over an hour without fidgeting. It was the first time that I felt so comfortable after two years of illness.

"I began to be convinced that Qi Gong was really capable of curing disease. I sat down at once to write a seven-page report to my coach describing my experience and my achievements.

"Since then, I've become more confident of the validity of Qi Gong. I have therefore continued to practice assiduously. From April 7 to June 7 in the short space of two months, I had achieved unhoped for results. All my symptoms disappeared. I felt vigorous and stable. I could sit and write for any length of time and I could work as never before. After July 1982, I went back to a full work schedule including work meetings, banquets, and conferences. I never seemed to be short of energy.

"In 1983, apart from my work, in my spare time I translated two books and published over forty articles. I attended the National Translators' Conference. During the conference I slept an average of three hours a day, but without ill effects.

"I know that I owe all this to Qi Gong. Qi Gong has allowed me to regain my health and to give greater contribution to China's dealings with foreign countries."

ARTERIOSCLEROSIS AND ATHEROSCLEROSIS

Both these conditions involve the partial occlusion of the arteries which, if left untreated, can lead to high blood pressure, impotence, coronary disease, heart attacks, and strokes. Arteriosclerosis is caused by the buildup of calcium on the inside of the artery wall, atherosclerosis by that of fat.

Both conditions are best treated through a correct diet: eliminating calcium and/or fats, avoiding sugar and salt and increasing the intake of fiber. Cayenne pepper and raw garlic appear to have some beneficial effect on arterial deposits as does raw, extra-virgin olive oil.

Pranayama and Qi Gong exercises are useful in that they promote improved circulation and increase the amount of oxygen in the blood thus facilitating the elimination of arterial deposits.

Nei Dan Qi Gong followed by Ba Duan Jin (Eight Pieces of Brocade) Qi Gong (see pages 110-120) are specific for arteriosclerosis.

See also the section on heart diseases in this chapter for general circulation therapy.

ARTHRITIS, RHEUMATOID, AND OSTEOARTHRITIS

Before discussing the effects of arthritis and related joint conditions, consider the case of Liu Han Min, fifty-six years old when he started Qi Gong in 1983, retired, from Beijing, who suffered from gastroptosis, osteoarthritis, asthma, low blood pressure, and various disorders of the heart, lungs, kidneys, liver, and spleen. His osteoarthritis is only one ailment out of many that was improved through the practice of Qi Gong.

Liu Han Min retired from work in 1964 at the age of thirty-seven for reasons of ill health. He had tuberculosis in his right lung, a peptic ulcer, and was suffering from heart, spleen, kidney, and liver disorders of various nature. His stomach was displaced by twelve inches and, finally, the fingers of both his hands were beginning to be deformed by arthritis. He could not eat, sleep, or walk properly. For the next few years, Liu spent at least one quarter of every year in the hospital. He was cured of tuberculosis and the ulcer but his other problems grew worse. In 1972 he had pulmonary emphysema. In 1975 he developed asthma which frequently left him unable either to walk or to speak.

Despite all this, Liu Han Min somehow survived another ten years. In 1982, he suffered a bronchial hemorrhage and lost his hearing as a result of the treatment. In 1983 he was plagued by asthma for five months. His blood pressure went down to 80 systolic and 50 diastolic.

Finally, in 1983, he resorted to Qi Gong.

"I started with Tai Ji Quan but was obliged to abandon it shortly afterward because of my lack of strength. On May 15, 1984, I tried a static, less fatiguing Qi Gong therapy. Three days later I felt a tingling sensation similar to an electric current in my hands. Then, a week later, I felt the Qi increasing in my hands during the exercise. There were waves of warmth rising from my hands up my arms and shoulders. I began to feel stronger. This encouraged me to continue with Qi Gong.

"On June 11 and 12, 1984, I twice felt a tightness around my head, like a strap. It lasted for ten minutes. After that my health improved dramatically. I no longer caught colds, I had a better appetite, and slept well.

"After ten months of Qi Gong, I had a general checkup on March 30, 1985. My stomach had risen by six inches, my spleen was functioning better, my blood pressure was normal (70/120) and my asthma seemed to have disappeared.

"The winter of 1984 was the happiest of my life. In one year Qi Gong had given me a new life."

Rheumatoid arthritis attacks the synovial membranes of the joints, osteoarthritis, the bones. Both diseases are degenerative and deforming and eventually affect the mobility of the limbs and joints. Their causes are hereditary, although cold, humidity, a faulty diet, and emotional repression contribute to worsening the effects of these diseases.

Remedial therapy is based on medication, heat application, and movement-extending exercises.

Qi Gong and Pranayama are useful in the treatment of arthritic diseases insofar as they exert a positive effect on the practitioner's general health. Yoga asana therapy, on the other hand, acts specifically on the joints and ligaments thus providing one of the best remedies for the disease. A full daily sitting of asanas for this purpose should include: Gomukhasan (the Cow), Halasana (the Plow), Bhujangasana (the Cobra), Dhanurasana (the Bow), Vrikshanasana (the One Legged Stand), Uttanpadasana (leg raising), and Ardha-Matsyendrasana (the Spinal Twist). See Chapter 7 for descriptions of these asanas.

Qi Gong exercises which loosen up the joints in a similar manner are the Eight Brocade Ba Duan Jin series and Tai Ji Quan.

Twenty minutes of deep breathing in the Qi Gong standing position with arms outstretched is also said to help.

ASTHMA, BRONCHIAL

Asthma is usually hereditary in nature. It is characterized by attacks of coughing and wheezing and gasping for breath usually brought on by an allergic reaction to pollen, animal dander, mold spores, or foodstuffs.

No yogic or Qi Gong remedy is available during an attack of asthma. The only treatment at such times is the administration of antihistamines such as epinephrine, and, in the most acute cases, of oxygen. The treatment of asthma through breathing techniques is possible only when the asthmatic's respiration is normal. Breathing techniques should, moreover, be combined with the observation of certain rules concerning lifestyle and diet. These are the same as those mentioned previously for allergies and hay fever.

Keep well away from the source of your particular allergy. If you are allergic to cats, get rid of the cat; if it's something in your diet that sets off your asthma, find out what it is, and stop eating it. However, not all allergens may be eliminated so easily; dust and pollen being the most obvious examples. It is advisable, in these cases, to prepare for the allergic reaction by cultivating a relaxed and optimistic attitude. The contributory psychosomatic causes of asthma should not be underestimated. To counteract these, you should, therefore, practice deep breathing relaxation techniques: Nei Dan Qi Gong or Ujjayi Pranayama in either the lying or sitting position.

The dietary recommendations made for allergies apply to asthma as well. A wholesome low-fat diet based on cereals and raw vegetables is thus preferred.

The useful exercises when preparing for or recovering from an attack of asthma are Nei Dan Qi Gong, alternate nostril breathing, Ujjayi Pranayama, Kapalabhati, Bhastrika, and Suryabhedana (see chapter 5). These strengthen the respiratory system and remove congestion. Jalaneti and Sutraneti cleansing techniques should be practiced every day when an attack of asthma is expected.

Jalaneti with cold unsalted water, with a 50 percent solution of milk and with a 25 percent solution of honey as described in the section on hay fever has also been shown to work.

Useful yoga asanas in combating asthma are Ekpa Uttanasana (breath retention with leg raising, see page 85), and Tarasana arm raising. Sarvangasana (the Candle Stand), Matsyasana (the Fish), and Padmasana (the Lotus pose) will also help. A daily round of either Tai Ji Quan or one of the Wai Dan forms of Qi Gong is equally useful. The case of Liu Han Min quoted previously (see page 147) illustrates how asthma, besides as a host of other ailments, was apparently cured by regular practice of Qi Gong.

BACKACHE AND SCIATICA

The causes may be overwork, postural defects, or rheumatic problems. The remedies include: exercise, Tai Ji Quan, Ba Duan Jin stretching, and Padmasana or Siddhasana postures as frequently as possible. Halasana (the Plow), Shalabhasana (the Locust), Gomukhasana (the Cow), and Paschimottanasana forward stretching Hatha yoga positions will also help. Dhanurasana (the Bow) massages the muscles of the back and Matsyasana (the Fish) removes stiffness from the cervical and lumbar regions of the spine.

BRONCHITIS, CHRONIC

The chronic inflammation of the lower part of the windpipe going into the lungs is usually due to a neglected bronchial infection. Chronic bronchitis is usually aggravated by damp, cold air, air pollution, and smoking. Prolonged infection leads to loss of elasticity of the breathing apparatus as a whole.

All forms of breathing exercises may be used to counteract the lack of bronchial elasticity.

A daily fifteen-minute stint of Pranayama or Qi Gong is sufficient. Kapalabhati on its own will help, too. Jala and sutra Neti cleaning should be practiced at least twice a week. Useful Hatha yoga asanas include Sarvangasana (the Candle Stand), Matsyasana (the Fish), Yoga Mudra (the symbol of yoga), and Tarasana.

CANCER

The precise causes of cancer are still unknown. The fact that certain cells in the body should begin reproducing in a disordered and uncontrolled manner, thus giving rise to a tumorous growth, has been linked by researchers to viral infection, irradiation, environmental and chemical pollution (including cigarette smoke), diet, and stress.

In order to reduce one's chances of cancer, which kills over 500,000 people a year in America alone, it would seem reasonable to protect oneself from the possible causes. One would therefore be well advised to choose a healthy natural environment free from pollution and far away from nuclear power plants, to stop smoking, to consume a diet which is low in animal fats and proteins and high in nuts, fiber, fruits and vegetables, and, finally, to reduce stress through Pranayama, yoga, and Qi Gong exercise.

If cancer has already been diagnosed there is still no reason to despair. Millions of people live long and useful lives in spite of the disease. Besides surgery, the main factors responsible for healthy survival are a positive attitude, diet, and exercise.

An anti-cancer diet should include beta-carotene, vitamin B complex, C and E supplements, raw onion, garlic, and almonds in addition to whole-grain wheat, corn, brown rice, oatmeal, nuts, broccoli, sprouts, cabbage, and cauliflower, plenty of yellow fruits and vegetables (carrots, melons, pumpkin, papaya, mangoes, peaches) as well as apples, berries, grapes, beans, lentils, and soy products. It should not include fried and junk foods, alcohol, coffee, tea (except unfermented green tea), candy, refined sugar, dairy products, and animal fats and proteins.

An anecdote from my own experience while working with Dr. Kutty Varier from Kerala, an Indian Ayurvedic doctor practicing in Italy in 1984, may illustrate the importance of eliminating animal protein from one's diet.

When she first visited Dr. Varier in 1983, Mrs. Barabino was suffering from a large tumorous growth in the neck which interfered both with her speech and mobility. The doctor prescribed two or three Ayurvedic products as well as a stringent vegetarian diet. During the first two months there was no further growth of the sarcoma, by the third month it had actually begun to decrease. After five months Mrs. Barabino had recovered mobility of her neck and her speech. The sarcoma had shrunk to the size of an egg. After six months the cancer began to grow, once again affecting her speech.

"Have you been taking your medicines?" asked Dr. Varier.

"Yes."

"Have you continued with the diet I prescribed for you?"

"Yes."

"No meat?"

"No."

"In that case, can you describe your diet to me in detail?"

"I eat brown rice, steamed, lightly boiled vegetables, fresh fruit, and occasionally a little ham —that's not considered meat, is it?"

Once the ham had been eliminated, Mrs. Barabino's tumorous growth receded and, in a matter of months, disappeared. Although there may have been other factors involved in this case and granted that a single example does not constitute proof of general efficacy, Mrs. Barabino's experience does seem to point toward the possibility that the consumption of meat may have a negative effect on cancer patients.

Another factor which appears to inhibit the growth of tumorous cells is exercise, in particular Qi Gong. The following account is taken from a 1987 publication of the Chinese Qi Gong Scientific Research Institute of Beijing.

Wu Gui Qu, retired, was suffering from cancer of the colon, arthritis, and severe neurasthenia.

Wu Gui Qu's cancer was first diagnosed at the end of 1978. On March 17, 1979, she underwent surgery for the removal of a section of her colon. After the operation, she continued to suffer from anemia and her bodily weight dropped from 110 pounds to 70 pounds.

By 1983 cancer had spread through the whole of Wu Gui Qu's digestive system.

"The doctor didn't say a word when I went to see him. He just showed me the x-rays. I could see that my abdomen was spotted with shadows the size of goose eggs. Then the doctor said that I was very fortunate to have survived this long, and that a second operation would be pointless.

"I was very depressed, but I refused to give up, so I went to another hospital where they treated me for three months with Chinese herbal medicines. It was there that I first heard about Qi Gong. I saw patients who became stronger because of it, and I grew interested.

"On June 9, 1983, I enrolled in the hospital's Qi Gong course. I did everything the instructor told me to do and kept at it. For three months I practiced Qi Gong three or four times a day.

"The results were amazing. After only two weeks, my x-rays showed that the tumors in my abdomen had shrunk to the size of hen's eggs. After one and a half months, they were just specks. Another six weeks later, they had disappeared.

"I was checked by three doctors independently of one another and all pronounced me cured. What's more, my arthritis was improving, too.

"After seven months of Qi Gong practice, I stopped taking medicines. Since then I have no longer been to hospital, but have continued doing my Qi Gong every day.

"Now (in 1987) I weigh 120 pounds. I am energetic, I regularly do the housework. My urine and blood tests are normal."

The Qi Gong practiced by Wu Gui Qu appears to have been straightforward Nei Dan breathing in the standing position (see page 92 or 128).

CARDIOVASCULAR DISEASES: See the Heart and Circulation

COLITIS OR INFLAMMATION OF THE COLON

Colitis may be either acute or chronic. In either case it is characterized by abdominal pain and diarrhea. The usual causes are poor diet, allergy to certain foods, and stress.

Two natural treatments are available: diet and exercise that act on the abdomen and digestive tract.

An anti-inflammatory diet consists of bland lightly boiled or steamed vegetables, well-cooked rice, oatmeal porridge, and bran. Grain, seeds, nuts, meat, sugar, fried food, and dairy products should not be eaten. Fruit should be taken either cooked or in juice form. An occasional fast may also help.

Exercises that massage the abdomen will tone up the inner organs and improve digestion. Therefore practice Uddiyana Bandha (see page 45), Kapalabhati (see page 53), Bhastrika (see page 55), Ujjayi Pranayama (see page 58), and Moorcha (see page 61). Abdominal stretching asanas such as Bhujangasana (see page 77) and Chakrasana (see page 84) will help.

Nei Dan abdominal breathing in either sitting or standing position has been known to help.

THE COMMON COLD

Everyone suffers from the common cold and from its accompanying congestion of the nose and upper respiratory tract. The best relief is to clear the mucous membranes by cleansing them daily with Jalaneti and Sutraneti. The variations of Jalaneti using cold unsalted water or milk and honey (see page 163) might also prove useful. Once the nasal passage has been cleared, three or four rounds of Bhastrika or Kapalabhati followed by twenty rounds of Suryabhedana, the Awakening Sun Breath (see page 59), a day should keep the cold away.

CONSTIPATION

For optimum health, the bowels should be cleared daily. Fecal matter which stays in the intestines for longer than twenty-four hours causes harmful bacteria to spread through the system. Furthermore, chronic constipation can lead to abdominal pain, diverticulitis, hemorrhoids, headaches, insomnia, digestive problems, obesity, circulatory problems, hernia, and cancer of the bowel.

A diet of fresh raw green-leaf vegetables, fruit, and plenty of fiber helps easy bowel movement. Plenty of water (drunk hot in China), or pure fruit juice, is needed to dissolve the added intake of fiber. Sweet potatoes boiled with sugar and ginger as well as steamed eggplant are specific Chinese remedies. For a laxative one would do well to stick to prunes—or try a Chinese decoction consisting of one teaspoon of honey with a few drops of sesame oil mixed in a glass of hot water to be drunk before bed. Chemical laxatives will clean out the intestines too thoroughly of all bacteria thus giving rise to chronic constipation.

To prevent constipation it is important to exercise. Any exercise will do because all physical activity helps move waste matter through the intestines. However, Pranayama's abdominal breathing techniques will prove particularly useful. Uddiyana Bandha is recommended as are the Jivha and Jalandhara Bandhas (see pages 47 and 44 respectively) with the accompanying tightening of the rectal muscles. Nei Dan Qi Gong Small Circulation, which includes similar tightening, is also useful.

The most effective yoga asanas for loosening the bowels are: Sarvangasana (the Candle Stand), Bhujangasana (the Cobra), Dhanurasana (the Bow), Yoga Mudra, and Pawanmuktasana (the Air Liberating position).

The Qi Gong remedy consists of the Ba Duan Jin Eight Brocade sequence of exercises followed by Nei Dan deep breathing in the standing position.

One variation of the Qi Gong standing position specifically for constipation is to stand with back straight and knees slightly bent as usual (see page 92 or 128), place hands on hips, and rotate the pelvis to the left, front, right, and back (clockwise) for five to ten minutes in the morning.

CROHN'S DISEASE, OR INFLAMMATION OF THE DIGESTIVE TRACT

What is said about colitis (see page 152) also applies to Crohn's disease. Crohn's disease is a noninfectious inflammation of the intestinal wall. Symptoms include diarrhea, cramps, pain in the lower right abdomen, fever, anemia, lethargy, and weight loss. Attacks appear to be brought on by stress.

Treatment consists of abdominal massage and stress-reducing exercises, such as may be treated by reducing stress and making sure that the bowels move daily.

As for colitis, Uddiyana Bandha (see page 45), Kapalabhati (see page 53), Bhastrika (see page 55), Ujjayi Pranayama (see page 58), and Moorcha (see page 61) offer some relief. Abdominal stretching asanas such as Bhujangasana (see page 77) and Chakrasana (see page 84) will also be of benefit.

Relaxation exercises in Shavasanaor one of the seated poses will help to reduce stress.

Nei Dan abdominal breathing in either sitting or standing position together with Ba Duan JinQi Gong (see pages 110-120).

DEPRESSION

Symptoms of depression include fatigue, insomnia, or too much sleep, poor appetite, headaches, colon disorders, and general feelings of worthlessness. Although causes can range from loneliness to thyroid disorders and physical illness, depression is usually susceptible to treatment by breathing therapy and yoga.

Depression is fundamentally a problem of mood. Any activity which acts directly on mood will, therefore, help in its cure. Sitting in the bright morning sunshine is known to be beneficial. Travel, socializing, learning, or taking an interest in some new activity can also help.

Pranayama and Qi Gong provide the depressed person with a novel exercise. Furthermore, the increase in oxygen consumption resulting from breathing exercises causes endorphins to be manufactured by the body. Endorphins exert a calming influence on the cerebral cortex; they actively combat depression by to inducing a state of natural well-being.

For best results, followed by Ujjayi Pranayama or Nei Dan Grand Circulation, Qi Gong in the standing position (see page 92 or 128) should be performed outdoors in bright morning sunshine. Barring this, try to practice in a well ventilated and brightly lit room.

DIABETES

Anyone with a history of diabetes in the family would be advised to start practicing Qi Gong and yoga as a preventive measure as early as possible. Diabetes is caused by a malfunction of the pancreas which stops producing sufficient insulin to convert dietary sugars into glycogen—glycogen being the only form of sugar which the body is capable of using and storing.

Although breathing exercises can give only little help to counteract the disease once it is manifest, their effects on the pancreas will ensure that this organ functions better than would otherwise be the case.

A full preventive course of Pranayama and yoga consists of: three to five rounds of Kapalabhati, followed by ten rounds of external kumbhaka (holding the breath out—see page 53) and by twenty rounds of alternate nostril breathing to be practiced twice a day, every day, morning and evening. This should be combined with the following asanas to be performed either before or after the Pranayama: Uttanpadasana (leg raising), Bhujangasana (the Cobra), Shalabhasana (the Locust), Paschimottanasana (forward stretch), Dhanurasana (the Bow), Pawanmuktasana with both legs together, and, finally, Shavasana (the Corpse posture). See chapter 7 for further details on these postures.

Qi Gong therapy for diabetes starts with five or ten minutes of Nei Dan breathing in the lying position. Qi should be made to accumulate in the Dan Tian by concentrating the attention on this point below the navel. Nei Dan should be followed by one of the Wai Dan Eight Brocade exercises. Zhong Li's Ba Duan Jin (see page 117) is particularly recommended. It is relaxing and includes a lower back massage (Exercise 4) which is said to be beneficial to diabetics. The lumbar massage (see page 103), followed by a foot massage (see page 104) may also be practiced to advantage. A daily two-hundred-yard Qi Gong walk (Xing Bu Gong— see page 130) is also advised.

It is, of course, unnecessary to emphasize that the proper low-sugar diet for diabetics cannot be discontinued simply because one is undergoing Qi Gong or yoga therapy.

An interview with one Han Zhao Ming, translated from a 1987 publication of the Chinese Qi Gong Scientific Research Institute of Beijing might be of interest.

Han Zhao Ming was already suffering from kidney and gall stones when he developed diabetes in 1981. He started practicing Qi Gong later that same year.

His blood sugar count before starting Qi Gong was 380 mg. % on an empty stomach. His urine sugar was at level number 5.

"I used to drink and eat a lot every day, but I never had any energy and I became despondent.

"When some neighbors told me about Qi Gong, I decided to try it immediately. The next morning I was at the Ba Yi Lake Park at five o'clock. They told me that the group was already full and that I would have to try elsewhere, but I insisted and was finally accepted.

"Every day I went out there to practice despite my weakness. After a few days I began to feel better until, one day, I got scared when my body started moving and shaking uncontrollably. My coach said that it was a good sign because it meant a strengthening of my Qi.

"Then I started doing deep breathing meditation. I often felt myself floating over an endless sea. I felt dreamy. Sometimes I had sort of visions, like the sun rising in the east, or green fields and birds singing. It felt very comfortable.

"Gradually my health improved. I felt stronger. I was no longer afraid of the cold. I started to urinate less frequently and I was less troubled by thirst. Before that, I had always felt that my mouth was dry and I had to drink continuously because of it. My urine became clearer, too.

"I had always used to be tired and lethargic in the mornings, now I get up at 5:00 A.M. every day.

"My blood sugar count had been 380 mg. % when I started Qi Gong. After only two weeks it was down to 240 mg. %. After a month it was 145 mg. % which is normal. I stopped taking medication for diabetes after that.

"Over the next five years, diabetes never troubled me again and the stones in my gall-bladder and kidney stopped bothering me. I have, what's more, never caught a cold since I started doing Qi Gong."

DIVERTICULITIS

Little less than a century ago, diverticulitis used to be one of those rare conditions that doctors had heard about but seldom seen. In India and China it still is, because diverticulitis is brought about by a diet high in processed, low-fiber foods and by stress. Today 50 percent of the population of Western Europe and the United States over the age of sixty suffer from diverticulitis.

Diverticuli are small pouches or sacs along the wall of the large intestine brought about by inflammation of the mucous membrane of the colon. When fecal matter is trapped within the diverticuli, these become infected. Severe pain can result.

Treatment of diverticulitis is the same as that for constipation: a high-fiber diet, plenty of liquids, and exercise (see page 153).

The specific exercises are Uddiyana, Jivha, and Jalandhara Bandhas (see pages 45, 47, and 44 respectively) with the accompanying tightening of the rectal muscles. Nei Dan Qi Gong Small Circulation, which includes similar tightening, is also useful.

The most effective yoga asanas for loosening the bowels are: Bhujangasana (the Cobra), Dhanurasana (the Bow), Yoga Mudra, and Pawanmuktasana (see chapter 7).

The Qi Gong remedy consists of the Ba Duan Jin Eight Brocade sequence of exercises followed by Nei Dan deep breathing in the standing position. The circular pelvic rotation described on page 153 can also help.

DRUG DEPENDENCY (SUBSTANCE ABUSE)

No one in their senses would practice yoga, Pranayama, and Qi Gong exercises for optimum health while at the same time damaging one's body with drugs, alcohol, or cigarettes.

All drugs are damaging to some extent, be they tobacco, heroin, marijuana, tranquilizers, or caffeine. Quite apart from the psychological effects of dependency, drugs are detrimental to the body's ordinary functions. They interfere with the absorption of nutrients from food, with hormonal secretions and balances, and they cause havoc with the immune system. Some are cancer inducing—marijuana contains the same carcinogens as tobacco, but in larger quantities.

Breaking a dependency is difficult. In some cases, heroin being the prime example, it is impossible without hospitalization or, at least, professional medical aid.

It is, first of all, a matter of will. A person must want to leave the drug behind in order to continue with a full and healthy life. The strategy, once the decision has been made, is to steer away from circumstances which create the urge or, perhaps, simply remind a person of the old habit. If you are in the habit of smoking an after-dinner cigarette with coffee, give up the coffee. If you associate the drug with people or places, stay away from them.

A person should flush out the toxins still in the body from the drug, and drink plenty of water and fresh fruit juices. Fasting is also recommended. After the fast, one should eat fresh, wholesome food and stick to it (for more about diet and fasting, please refer to chapter 3). Practicing Kapalabhati or Bhastrika and Ujjayi Pranayama for at least twenty minutes every day is most beneficial. Keeping the body active with yoga asanas or with Wai Dan Qi Gong is also recommended. One should relax with Shavasana or Nei Dan Qi Gong in the lying position.

Above all, keep at it and never despair. With an optimistic attitude, a healthy diet, and the physical activity of Qi Gong or yoga and Pranayama, it takes only a matter of months to recover full healthy independence from toxic substances.

See also Alcoholism.

DIGESTIVE TRACT INFLAMMATION: See Crohn's Disease

DYSPEPSIA OR POOR APPETITE

Dyspepsia is a general lack of appetite which leads to lazy eating, poor digestion, and accompanying flatulence, nausea, and constipation. Its most frequent cause is lack of exercise.

Any form of exercise is considered a remedy. Wai Dan Qi Gong, yoga, and Pranayama in all their forms will stimulate a good appetite and thus ensure better digestion.

Yoga and Qi Gong teachers assert that when poor appetite is a problem, it is preferable to consume frequent highly nutritious and easily digestible snacks throughout the say rather than adhere to the usual regime of two or three meals.

EATING DISORDERS: ANOREXIA AND BULIMIA

Anorexia

Anorexia nervosa is the pathological terror of becoming fat. Affecting mostly teenage females, it is characterized by the refusal to eat food (often accompanied by forced vomiting, though not always) and extreme thinness. For those people who do not recover from this eating disorder—about one person in three—anorexia frequently leads to deficiency disorders, amenorrhea, and, on occasion, premature death.

Anorexia is fundamentally psychological in origin. It frequently is derived from feelings of insecurity and low self-esteem. One of the main impediments to successful treatment is the lack of voluntary participation in therapy on the patient's part. A positive and understanding attitude within the family is thus a precondition to treatment. The patient's appreciation of the problem followed by psychotherapy will, in most cases, guarantee recovery.

Pranayama and Qi Gong therapy can serve as useful correlative treatments. The calming effect of deep breathing exercises, their efficacy in correlating the endocrine and thyroid systems, and the sense of purpose and discipline involved in their daily practice will all help the anorexic to come to terms with his or her condition.

For best results, the anorexic patient should be persuaded that an easy course of yoga and Pranayama (see page 69) or Nei Dan Grand Circulation Qi Gong in the standing pose, followed by self-massage and Ba Duan Jin will help the anorexic achieve greater fitness and strength.

Bulimia

Bulimia involves the overconsumption of food, in the form of bingeing and purging. The basic psychological issues leading to the condition are often similar to those of the anorexic patient. As a consequence, treatment of the two disorders is usually the same.

Ravenous and uncontrollable hunger lead the bulimic patient to overeat, usually to the point of vomiting. Food consumption is pathological and obsessive. Without eating, the bulimic complains of excessive weakness and lethargy. As a result, cravings are principally for low-nutrient, short-burst energy foods such as sugars and sweets. The consequent increase in body fat frequently leads the patient to obsessive, calorie-burning exercise, and induces a sense of personal inadequacy.

Therapy, Twelve-Step groups, and developing a positive attitude toward oneself are the best remedies. Inducing a bulimic to take steps toward a treatment is often less arduous than in the case of anorexia. Therefore the therapeutic effects of Pranayama and Qi Gong exercises can work effectively against this condition. If practiced regularly they exert a calming influence on the psyche, are able to restore any imbalances in the thyroid and endocrine systems, and, last but not least, provide an opportunity for introspection and increasing self-esteem.

The short course of Pranayama and yoga (see page 68) or twenty minutes a day of Nei Dan Grand Circulation in the standing position (see page 92 or 128) will afford the necessary stimulus as well as affecting any glandular or metabolic imbalances.

See Obesity.

EMPHYSEMA

Emphysema is caused by loss of elasticity of the tissues of the lungs. Its symptoms are difficulty in breathing, breathlessness with the slightest exertion, and coughing. The condition is gradual, usually starting in middle age and becoming serious in later life. The most common cause is smoking although deficiency in serum protein and poorly treated pulmonary diseases are sometimes responsible.

Although total recovery of lung elasticity is not possible, regular practice of Kapalabhati (see page 53), followed by Ujjayi with kumbhaka breath retention (see page 58) will ensure that pulmonary efficiency is maximized. Much coughing and discomfort will accompany the exercises to begin with. Nevertheless, it is only by exercising regularly that any headway at all can be made with this disease.

If Kapalabhati and kumbhaka prove too difficult, Nei Dan Qi Gong in the seated or, preferably, in the standing position, should be practiced instead.

FATIGUE AND CHRONIC FATIGUE

Chronic fatigue which is not attributable to an underlying physical condition is usually the result of high-fat diet, refined food, vitamin and mineral deficiency, and chronic stress.

Check with your doctor first for possible physical causes. These are many and may range from allergies to yeast infections, diabetes, EBV (Epstein Barr virus), or liver problems.

If the fatigue is not a symptom of something else, begin by improving your diet. Eliminate junk food and sugars. Eat plenty of raw vegetables, fruits, nuts, and whole-grain cereals. Drink pure water and pure fruit juices. For more information on healthy eating please refer to chapter 3.

The subsequent step is to exercise the lungs and to circulate the Qi. Nei Dan and Wai Dan Qi Gong (Ba Duan Jin, or Eight Pieces of Brocade, see pages 110-120) practiced on a daily basis are gentle enough exercises to tone up the system without further increasing fatigue.

Ujjayi Pranayama and three or four easy Yoga asanas (Sarvangasana, Tara asana, Halasana, and Bhujangasana—see chapter 7) are a valid alternative.

FLATULENCE

Flatulence is the technical name for a bloated stomach or intestinal tract due to the excessive formation of gas during digestion.

Too much gas is due to the fermentation or putrefaction of food, to disorders of the liver, to lack of adequate physical exercise and, often, to nervous tension.

Some foods, such as beans and chestnuts, form more gas than others during the process of digestion. There is little one can do but stay away from them. Sufferers

Figure 87: Shavasana shoulder stand variation

from flatulence should also cut down their intake of heavy fats and animal protein.

Apart from that, the only remedy is to exercise and to relax.

All forms of Qi Gong and yoga will help. They ensure physical activity and they relax the nerves. Bhujangasana is beneficial for the abdominal organs in general. By its very name, Pawanmuktasana, the Air Liberating position, is the specific remedy for the actual elimination of excess gas from the intestines. For obvious reasons, this exercise is best performed alone. The Shavasana shoulder stand is also helpful. A variation of the Shavasana shoulder stand, with the body bent in the middle and the arms holding up the knees, puts pressure on the abdomen and is thus particularly suitable for flatulence (see figure 87).

The specific Pranayama remedies for flatulence are alternate nostril breathing, Kapalabhati, and Uddiyana Bandha (see pages 53 and 45 respectively).

Qi Gong therapy will include Nei Dan breathing in the seated or lying position.

FRIGIDITY: See Sexual Weakness

GASTRITIS

Acute gastritis is caused either by food poisoning, infection, or by excessive eating or drinking. It appears and subsides rapidly and should be treated with sedatives and abstention from food. There is nothing Qi Gong or Pranayama can do.

Chronic gastritis, on the other hand, usually depends on the habitual heavy use of irritants such as chili and pepper in one's diet, and on psychosomatic causes such as anxiety, stress, and frustration.

The obvious solution is to eliminate the irritants and to relax.

The specific remedies are: Kapalabhati followed by alternate nostril breathing. Plavini or Bahiskrita Dhauti (see pages 62 and 63) may also be useful. Swallowing air does appear to give relief to acidity and indigestion. Vamana Dhauti may also be tried, if you feel up to it. This purification technique consists of drinking three or four glasses of lukewarm salty water before breakfast and of throwing it all up immediately afterwards by pushing your fingers down your throat. This may be done two or three times a week. See page 162 for the variation of Vamana Dhauti using a plastic tube.

The most suitable yoga asanas for gastritis are: Sarvangasana shoulder stand, Uttanpadasana leg raising, Pawanmuktasana freeing of gasses, Yoga Mudra, Bhujangasana (the Cobra), Shalabhasana (the Locust), Paschimottanasana forward stretching, and Shavasana relaxation.

Qi Gong therapies for chronic gastritis are based on the Eight Brocade Ba Duan Jin series of exercises with particular emphasis on the arm stretching Exercises 2 and 3 (see page 112) and forward stretching Exercise 6. Nei Dan Qi circulation in either the lying or sitting position should follow. Concentration on the Dan Tian below the navel and on the visualization of expanding to the gastric area is also said to help. One should finish off with a light massage over the abdominal area.

GASTRIC AND PEPTIC ULCERS

Stomach ulcers tend to affect 10 percent of all men and 2 percent of all women above the age of fifty. The classic early symptom is abdominal pain when one's stomach is empty. Filling the stomach banishes the pain, and frequent eating may relieve the symptom altogether. If, however, the ulcer progresses, later symptoms include vomiting, acidity in the breath and mouth, and blood in the stools and vomit. Treatment consists of antacid medications or surgery.

Peptic and gastric ulcers are sometimes related to the onset of some pulmonary and nervous system diseases. However, in the majority of cases, they are attributable to high levels of stress, fatigue, and emotional tension.

Because of their proven beneficial effects on the emotions and nerves, Pranayama and Qi Gong should, therefore, be practiced as a preventive measure by anyone at risk of developing gastric or peptic ulcers. When, however, an ulcer is already present, breathing techniques can still prove useful. All forms of breathing exercises, including kumbhaka breath retention, exert a regulatory effect upon the digestive and nervous systems. They will thus help to regulate the acid secretions of the stomach, improve digestion, and counteract the underlying causes behind the formation of the ulcer.

Qi Gong therapy, in the case of ulcers, consists of Nei Dan breathing either lying or sitting while visualizing the accumulation of Qi in the Dan Tian and surrounding area. A light massage over the abdomen should follow.

In yoga therapy, cleansing the stomach is recommended. There are two ways to go about this: Vamana Dhauti and Vastra Dhauti.

Vamana Dhauti consists of cleansing the stomach by drinking three or four glasses of warm salty water and then eliminating it either by vomiting (by pushing your fingers down your throat), or by swallowing a three-foot-long plastic tube until its end protrudes from the mouth, then leaning forward far enough for the salt water to come up the tube and out. Most people throw up before the tube is six inches down the throat. However, anyone who can do it without retching their guts out, might wish to try Vastra Dhauti as well. All one has to do for this one is to swallow a four-foot-long strip of cotton cloth moistened in water. One end must always stay out of the mouth because, once swallowed, the cloth has to be pulled very slowly out again. The idea is to absorb all excess acid inside the stomach. Care must be taken never to keep the cloth in your stomach for more than ten minutes. After that time, digestion will have begun and you'll never get the cloth out again without doing something nasty to your insides.

Vamana Dhauti should be practiced two or three times a week; Vastra Dhauti not more than once a week. However, before partaking in any form of stomach cleansing, it is necessary that you consult your doctor.

Suitable yoga positions which give some relief to ulcer sufferers are the same as those for gastritis, namely: Sarvangasana shoulder stand, Uttanpadasana raising, Pawanmuktasana freeing of gasses, Yoga Mudra, Bhujangasana (the Cobra),

Shalabhasana (the Locust), Paschimottanasana forward stretching, and Shavasana relaxation. See chapter 7 for details.

GOUT

Although no longer a common ailment today, it is worth mentioning gout in this context because this disease is one of the most easily curable through yoga and Qi Gong therapy.

The disease arises when uric acid from a rich protein diet accumulates in the joints of the feet and hands causing pain and swelling. The remedy is to 1) eliminate excess protein from one's diet, and 2) exercise the joints and limbs sufficiently to relieve the accumulated uric acids. The most effective asanas are those which are performed upside down: Shirshasana (the Head Stand), and Sarvangasana (the Candle Stand). The latter exercise coupled to the cycling movement of the feet is particularly effective.

Other useful exercises are those affecting the synovial joints such as Gomukhasana (the Cow), Bhujangasana (the Cobra), Vrikshanasana (the One-Legged Stand), and Ekpada Uttanasana (single leg raising) in the standing position—see chapter 7. One of the Ba Duan Jin forms of Qi Gong is equally valid (see pages 110-120).

HAY FEVER OR ALLERGIC RHINITIS

What has been said above about allergies in general refers also to hay fever.

The additional techniques that are useful for combating hay fever are regular cleaning of the nasal passages by means of Jalaneti and Sutraneti (see pages 27-28) and some good hard alternate nostril Bhastrika cleansing (see page 55).

Jalaneti (nasal cleansing with water) is normally done with salted lukewarm water. In cases of allergic rhinitis, however, Jalaneti may be performed with cold, unsalted water, with milk and with honey.

Jalaneti with cold, unsalted water: By gradually decreasing water temperature and salt content the mucous membranes in the nose will develop resistance to variations in temperature and environmental irritants.

Jalaneti with diluted milk Each day add ever-increasing quantities of milk to the water used for nasal cleansing until you have a 50 percent solution after two weeks. Milk Jalaneti is said to develop resistance in the nasal mucous membranes against proteins.

Jalaneti with honey: Gradually add honey to the lukewarm water for cleansing until you have a 25 percent solution after two weeks. Jalaneti with honey develops resistance against pollen grains in the air.

Patients with cough and catarrh should practice Kapalabhati (page 53) and Bhastrika (page 55). As an additional cleansing therapy, Vastra Dhauti (see page 162, Gastric and Peptic Ulcers) might also be attempted.

Of 124 hay fever sufferers treated for two to four weeks with the above Jalaneti variations at the Kaivalyadhama Institute in Lonavla, eighty-seven (70 percent) had no allergic attack during treatment and subsequently showed an all round improvement. Twenty-three patients (18.5 percent) had no attacks during treatment although no significant improvement resulted afterward. Four suffered mild attacks during treatment but did improve their general resistance to pollen later. Ten could not complete the treatment because of other illness.

The above cleansing methods also help in cases of bronchial asthma, sinusitis, bronchitis, and chronic cold.

HEADACHES

The causes of headaches can be anything from eye strain to stress, a poor night's rest or the common cold. Whatever the cause, all deep breathing exercises will offer some relief. Try half a minute of Kapalabhati followed by twenty rounds of slow deep breathing without kumbhaka breath retention. Regular practice of Jalaneti may give relief. Nei Dan breathing either standing, sitting, or lying, followed by a head and face massage (see page 100) will afford relief in all but the most stubborn cases.

THE HEART AND HEART AILMENTS: CORONARY THROMBOSIS, DEGENERATIVE HEART DISEASE, HYPERTENSIVE HEART DISEASE

It must be stressed that yogic breathing therapies and Qi Gong afford little help during the acute stage of a heart disease such as during a heart attack or a thrombosis. However, it has been found at the Indian Institute of Yoga in Patna and at the Kaivalyadhama Yoga Research Institute in Lonavla as well as at the Beijing College of Traditional Chinese Medicine that regular practice of Yoga or Qi Gong can bring most heart patients back to normal health within three to nine months, depending on the seriousness of the initial condition.

Yogic and Qi Gong therapy for heart diseases is usually divided into three phases. In the first phase, lasting from three weeks to three months, medication is primary and exercise only secondary. During this phase, exercise should be of the gentlest possible kind: Shavasana relaxation posture and gentle deep breathing. In phase two, lasting between two weeks and three months, medication is gradually diminished and, if possible, eliminated; exercise becomes primary. In the final stage (again, three weeks to three months), yoga or Qi Gong are used to consolidate the benefits already achieved. An adequate low-fat and low-animal protein diet with plenty of cereals, fresh fruit, and vegetables should accompany these therapies.

Phase One

Shavasana (the Corpse posture), or Nei Da Qi Gong in the lying position should be practiced two or three times a day for thirty or forty minutes at a stretch. Gentle deep breathing without breath retention should be accompany each sitting. One is ready for phase two only when the acute symptoms of heart disease (chest pains, chronic shortage of breath) have disappeared.

Phase Two

EITHER: Nei Dan Qi Gong in the sitting posture, followed either by exercise Eight of the Ba Duan Jin (rising and falling on the toes), by a gentle Tai Ji Quan session or by Da Mo's Wai Dan exercises, once or twice a day for thirty minutes each sitting. Each session should be completed with twenty minutes of deep breathing in the lying position. OR: Ten minutes of Pranayama in a sitting posture without breath retention twice a day, followed by six gentle rounds of Pawanmuktasana and Uttanpadasana in the lying position, followed by twenty minutes of Shavasana. For descriptions of Pawanmukta and Uttanpada asanas, please refer to pages 87 and 85 respectively.

During the second phase of treatment, deep breathing in the Shavasana lying position should still be practiced independently of the other exercises at least once a day.

Phase Three

EITHER: Fifteen minutes of Grand Circulation Nei Dan Qi Gong followed by one of the full Wai Dan Qi Gong techniques at least once a day. OR: Pranayama with only a very short breath retention between each inhalation and exhalation, followed by a short yoga therapy course (see chapter 6) and by ten minutes of Shavasana.

HEMORRHOIDS

Also known as piles, hemorrhoids are caused either by a genetic weakness of the veins in the rectum, by sedentary habits or by constipation. They are characterized by discomfort and sometimes pain, and by frequent bleeding from the rectum during defecation. They may either be internal or protrude from the body.

The best way to prevent piles is to exercise. Any exercise will do but, if constipation is responsible, Pranayama's abdominal breathing techniques will prove particularly useful. Uddiyana Bandha is recommended as are the Jivha and Jalandhara Bandhas with the accompanying tightening of the rectal muscles. Nei Dan Qi Gong Small Circulation, which includes similar tightening, is also useful.

A suitable low-fat, low-protein diet of fruits, greens, fiber, and yogurt must also form part of any therapy aimed at preventing hemorrhoids.

HYPERTENSION OR HIGH BLOOD PRESSURE

Normal blood pressure in a healthy adult is 120 mm Hg. when the lower chamber of the heart contracts to force the blood through the arteries (diastolic), and 80 mm Hg. on the rebound, when the same chamber expands to receive blood (systolic). These figures may increase slightly with age, but any significantly higher pressures (over 15 percent more than normal) may be considered dangerous to one's overall health. An abnormally high arterial blood pressure may have a variety of causes. It may be hereditary, or due to emotional tension, the hardening of the arteries, high cholesterol, kidney disease, a disease of the endocrine or the nervous systems, or any blockage of the arteries. In most cases, the cure for hypertension is effected by treating its underlying cause. When this cause is not apparent, as in "essential," or hereditary high blood pressure, it is usual treated by the administration of specific drugs.

The yogic remedy for essential hypertension is to relax.

Twenty minutes of Shavasana twice a day is ideal. Relaxation should be followed by fifteen minutes of Nei Dan Qi Gong or Pranayama according to preference. Moderate breath retention (kumbhaka) should be practiced for best results.

Qi Gong remedies for hypertension should start with ten to twenty minutes of Da Zhou Tian (Grand Circulation) Nei Dan Qi Gong followed by either the Eight or Twelve Pieces of Brocade exercises. The Head Turning, Drawing the Bow, and Slow Punching exercises (Exercises 1, 4, and 7) of the Ba Duan Jin should be repeated frequently for best results (see pages 110-117).

HYPERTHYROID/HYPOTHYROID

When the thyroid gland in the lower neck produces too much hormone (hyperthyroid) the body's metabolism works overtime leading to irritability, insomnia, and exhaustion. When the thyroid underproduces its hormone (hypothyroid) the results are lethargy, weakness, and fatigue. In either case Pranayama with kumbhaka breath retention in the Jalandhara chin-lock (see page 44) exerts a beneficial pressure on the thyroid gland in the neck. The Sarvangasana shoulder stand (the Candle stand) and the Matsyasana (the Fish) exert a similar beneficial pressure.

Other remedies are dietary.

If suffering from hyperthyroid eat plenty of raw cabbage, cauliflower, broccoli, brussels sprouts, soy products, spinach, turnips, peaches, and pears. Avoid dairy products for three months.

If suffering from hypothyroid—this is, in fact, a far more common condition than hyperthyroid—one should eat only small quantities of the above foods. A person should eat plenty of kelp and sushi—seaweed contains iodine, the basis of the thyroid hormone. Iodine supplement tablets may also be taken. Avoid fluoride and chlorine both of which are chemically similar to iodine and fool the thyroid gland into blocking its receptivity to vital iodine. Fluoride is in most toothpastes—use one without it. Chlorine is in most drinking water. Drink distilled water instead.

INSOMNIA

Insomnia is one of the common health problems which is most amenable to treatment through yoga, Pranayama, and Qi Gong therapy. In order to sleep, one must be able to relax. Oriental breathing techniques help one to do just that.

Laboratory studies on the effects of yoga therapy on habitual insomniacs[5] have shown that one month of practice of Pranayama, asanas, and meditation is sufficient to ensure a significant improvement in sleeping habits without the use of sleep-inducing drugs.

After ensuring that one's insomnia is not due to dietary deficiencies (lack of calcium and of magnesium cause insomnia) or to the consumption of caffeine, a suitable program to counteract this complaint should include fifteen to twenty minutes of keep fit exercises two to three hours before going to bed. Once in bed, ten to fifteen minutes of slow, deep breathing in either Shavasana (the Corpse posture) or the Qi Gong lying position (see pages 93 and 129), should ensure a good night's rest.

If, however, this also fails to send you to sleep, you may wish to get up and try the following Qi Gong remedy as a last resort:

1) Stand in the Qi Gong breathing position with knees bent and arms outstretched until you begin to sweat—usually for ten to twenty minutes.
2) Walk between one and two hundred paces in the manner described in chapter 10 (Xing Bu Gong).

3) Wash your feet and hands in hot water.
4) Massage the underside of your feet by pressing one hundred times on the soft point in the center of the foot where the toe bones end and the arch begins.
5) Go back to bed and try again.

IRRITABLE BOWEL

Inflammation of the bowel may depend on food allergies, an excess of nonsoluble fiber in the diet, pepper, chili, animal fats, and other irritants. The symptoms are abdominal pain accompanied by constipation or diarrhea, flatulence, and bloating.

The remedy is to eat a bland diet and to exert gentle massage on the intestines by practicing Uddiyana Bandha (see page 45) and Kapalabhati or Bhastrika. Zhong Li's Ba Duan Jin performed in the seated position entails abdominal stretching and massage (see pages 117-120).

MENSTRUAL PROBLEMS: See Uro-Genital Problems

MIGRAINE OR HEMICRANIA

Also known as hemicrania, a migraine usually arises in the temples, the forehead, or the eyes and diffuses to the whole head. It is often accompanied by increased visual sensitivity to light, nausea, dizziness, and irritability. Pain may last between two minutes and several days. The causes appear to be hereditary and generally depend on the constriction of the arteries carrying blood to the head.

The remedies: Exercises should be started only after the attack of a migraine is over. Nei Dan Qi Gong with head massages followed by Zhong Li's Ba Duan Jin is ideal. On the Pranayama side, twenty rounds of deep breathing without kumbhaka should be practiced twice a day. These may be preceded by half a minute of Kapalabhati and followed by a few rounds of Sitali without breath retention.

MULTIPLE SCLEROSIS

Multiple sclerosis is a progressive, degenerative disease which attacks the central nervous system causing to numbness, weakness, tremors, and eventually paralysis. Although its cause is unknown, the onset of the disease is usually characterized by an immune system weakened by stress or malnutrition. There exists no known cure for multiple sclerosis.

As for most degenerative ailments, Pranayama and Qi Gong afford relief by strengthening the body as a whole. Multiple sclerosis progresses through recurring, ever more devastating bouts of weakness, tremors, and paralysis of the limbs and muscles. Because they ensure efficient functioning of the digestive and metabolic systems, Pranayama and Qi Gong are extremely valuable in slowing down the progress of the disease. Furthermore, the gentle stretching and massaging exercises of yoga and Qi Gong help to prevent involuntary muscle contracting when crises do occur.

Yoga asanas which strengthen the nervous system as a whole are: Halasana (the Plow), Bhujangasana (the Cobra), Sarvangasana (the Candle Stand), Matsyasana (the Fish), Dhanurasana (the Bow), Paschimottanasana forward stretch, Chakrasana (the Wheel), Shirshasana head stand, and finally Shavasana relaxation or meditation for fifteen to twenty minutes. Please refer to chapter 7 for further details of these asanas.

Although Li Shang Jun, an officer in the Chinese Air Force, did not suffer from multiple schlerosis, in October 1979, when he was fifty years old, Li Shang Jun suffered a cerebral hemorrhage. He was paralyzed in the entire left half of his body and could only speak with difficulty, and suffered many of the same symptoms that multiple sclerosis patients do. Acupuncture and ultrasonic therapy gave marginal improvement allowing him some degree of mobility with the help of crutches. After one year he was able to drag himself around awkwardly without crutches or a stick. His story of recovery is remarkable.

"I heard about Qi Gong from a friend. There seemed no harm in giving it a try. To begin with, though, I couldn't even raise my arms and hands into the position. I couldn't bend my knees either. My instructor told me not to worry. The point is to do your best even if you can't adopt the right position. He told me that it was the mental attitude that counts. Sometimes I fell over. But I got to my feet again and kept at it. Gradually I began to feel some mild effects. After one week and five days of practice my body started moving of its own accord. It seemed so strange because movements that were normally impossible for me seemed to happen spontaneously. Now, because of this, I could feel some force within me twisting my upper body slowly to the right. I tried to resist, but it was stronger than my will. It stopped. Then this force twisted me back to the left. I can't remember how many times it happened. Then it bent me forward so that I could touch my toes. This stretching and twisting lasted about an hour. Afterward I felt relaxed.

"In the following months, spontaneous movement became a fairly frequent occurrence. Sometimes I'd move quite fast, jumping and waving my arms about with my feet kicking. With time, the spontaneous movements became milder and more

controllable. Two months later I could climb on and off the bus on my own. One year later I was capable of riding a bicycle over twenty kilometers. In the meantime my memory and reactions had improved. I could read, write, and talk without difficulty. My gait and my speech were totally different from before starting Qi Gong.

"I have benefited so greatly from Qi Gong that I would like as many people as possible to know about it and about what it did for me. I hope that more and more people will try it and let Qi Gong bring health back into their lives."

NEURASTHENIA

Neurasthenia is a generic term resorted to by members of the medical profession when they can't find anything wrong with a person. It is often used interchangeably with hypochondria. In spite of this, neurasthenia—which literally means "nervous weakness"—does manifest through a number of characteristic and troublesome symptoms. Neurasthenic patients usually complain of weakness, fatigue, diffuse pain through the body, irritability, and insomnia.

Because of the apparently psychosomatic nature of the complaint, neurasthenia is one of the ailments most easily cured by the relaxation and deep-breathing techniques of Pranayama, yoga, and Qi Gong. Daily practice allows the patient to introspect and come to terms with his or her own body. It recharges the "weak nerves" both physically and psychologically. It invigorates without exhausting. As a result, stubborn cases of psychosomatic disorders that have caused years of suffering have been known, under the effect of Qi Gong or yogic treatment, to clear up completely in a matter of weeks. The important point is to keep at it.

A few simple yoga exercises followed by ten minutes of Ujjayi Pranayama and five more minutes of meditation, every day, should be sufficient. Nei Dan Qi Gong circulation in either the seated or standing position is also of proven benefit.

Consider the case of forty-five-year-old Ma Mo, head radiologist at the General Hospital of Beijing for the Armed Forces, who suffered from neurasthenia since the early 1970s:

For fourteen years Ma Mo was unable to sleep, fitfully, for more than four hours each night. As a result he felt drowsy and dizzy during the day. At work he was unable to concentrate. He could no longer rely on his memory even for the simplest things. He suffered from nervousness, palpitations, and severe headaches. Twice, in November 1977 and in December 1978, Ma Mo had to be hospitalized in the neurological department of his own institution (his registration number— 17100—is given just in case you'd like to check!). Ma Mo's electroencephalographs results were normal and neurasthenia was therefore diagnosed.

Sodium bicarbonate injections were given him for ten days without results.

"All these years I had been taking a vast number of Chinese medicines to no effect. I had resorted to acupuncture and magnetic therapy with only slight and temporary improvement. Western medicine, tranquilizers, and sleeping pills made me drowsy at first. Later they appeared only to make my condition worse. At night I couldn't sleep, by day I was virtually incapacitated. Whenever I fell asleep I'd be woken up, minutes later, by nightmares. Palpitations followed. My legs were permanently painful and swollen. I resorted to sitting up in bed each night waiting for daybreak.

"My illness appeared to be incurable. I was thoroughly despondent. Finally, trusting entirely to chance, I tried Qi Gong as a last resort. I started to practice in 1984. At home I practiced three times a day for thirty minutes each sitting. After a few days I felt that my leg muscles were stronger; my whole body seemed lighter. About one week later I began to sleep slightly better, about five to six hours, though never continuously. During the second week of Qi Gong practice, when I concentrated on the Dan Tian [below the navel], I felt warmth spreading over my entire abdomen. With gentle to and fro movements of my arms I felt heat flowing along them. When my Qi Gong sessions were over it was as if a shapeless wave of liquid flowed from my hands. I felt comfortable.

During the third week, whenever I practiced Qi Gong I felt relaxed and happy. Qi Gong became a kind of enjoyment. Starting from the end of the third week I began to sleep properly. For two full weeks I slept well without nightmares, waking only occasionally and always able to go back to sleep afterwards with ease. After that I stopped taking tranquilizers and sleeping pills. Every morning I started day feeling relaxed and energetic. It became easy to concentrate again at work.

"All these years I had suffered. I could never have imagined that with a mere three weeks of Qi Gong practice I would have achieved such vast improvement. Since I now realize the value of Qi Gong I have kept it up ever since. A single day without practice and I feel uncomfortable. In December of 1984, only ten months after starting Qi Gong, I considered myself completely cured. Ever since I have felt healthier, more energetic, and capable of giving my contribution to our country's progress."

OBESITY

Obesity is usually due to overeating and lack of exercise. In about 5 percent of cases, its causes are hormonal imbalances or glandular defects. Obesity may not be a disease as such, it does, however, usually have serious consequences on general health. Obese people have a lower life expectancy than others, their resistance to disease is lower than normal and they are prone to degenerative diseases of the heart, the circulation and the kidneys, and to diabetes.

The remedies: In 95 percent of cases, cutting down on the intake of calories stimulates weight loss. (For information on healthy eating refer to chapter 3.) This is obviously more easily said than done. Diets may help temporarily, but the tendency to overeat will reassert itself in time. Overeating may depend on emotional deficiencies, loneliness, boredom, or a defect in the hunger regulating mechanism in the hypothalamus which forgets to turn itself off when one has had enough. Control of these factors requires a willpower and degree of self-control that few people have.

This is where Pranayama and Qi Gong can help. The mere fact of sitting down to a daily stint of exercise helps to keep up one's resolve. Second, breathing exercises actually seem to readjust the control mechanisms in the hypothalamus which regulate hunger. Thirdly, the calming influence of the exercises has a beneficial effect on the emotional deficiencies which may be causing the overeating.

The specific remedies are: forty rounds of Ujjayi with kumbhaka of at least ten seconds, followed by twenty rounds of Sitkari Pranayama (see pages 58 and 61), or ten to twenty minutes a day of breathing in the Qi Gong standing position (see page 92 or 128). Xing Bu Gong walking control (see page 132) is recommended as well as one of the Ba Duan Jin, Eight Pieces of Brocade Wai Dan Qi Gong. The yoga asanas to be preferred for obesity are: Sarvangasana (the Candle Stand), Bhujangasa (the Cobra), and Shalabhasa (the Locust).

In addition, developing the habit of taking long walks, and drinking water before each meal can help.

PERSONALITY DISORDERS

A heading such as this can include anything from schizophrenia to a smoking habit. The generalization is, however, deliberate. To paraphrase the famous Buddhist's dictum: "A bad action oft repeated becomes a habit, a bad habit in time becomes a personality disorder, a personality disorder carried through life becomes an unhappy destiny."[6]

It is not, therefore, so much a question of what a personality problem is, so much as how it affects and interferes with daily life. Whether the problem is nail biting, alcohol or drug abuse, or a full-blown psychosis, if it warrants taking corrective action, Pranayama and Qi Gong can help.

Adequate evidence exists, be it personal experience or laboratory experiment, to show that all disorders of the personality can be treated effectively by Pranayama, yoga, and Qi Gong. It is important to want enough to try and to persevere. With time, one gains new insights into oneself, renewed energy, stability and, with these, the optimism and the dynamism that lead to change.

See also Drug Dependency.

POSTURAL DEFECTS

Postural defects usually depend on the wrong distribution of bodily weight over the spinal column or, more simply, on not holding the back erect. Unless the defect is hereditary, or due to injury, the remedy consists of strengthening the back muscles and forming the habit of holding the spine straight.

Padmasana or Siddhasana postures both strengthen the back and force it to remain erect. Ordinary Pranayama with or without kumbhaka should be practiced for ten to fifteen minutes a day.

For strengthening the muscles of the lower back, the most potent Hatha yoga exercise is the Shalabhasana, or the Locust pose. For stretching and ensuring flexibility, Halasana (the Plow) should be practiced at least once a day. A full course of asanas designed to correct postural defects should start with Sarvangasana (the Candle) and should be followed by Halasana, Bhujangasana (the Cobra), Shalabhasana (the Locust), Dhanurasana (the Bow), Paschimottanasana (the Forward Stretch), Chakrasana (the Wheel), Matsyasana (the Fish), Yoga Mudra and, finally, by Ardha-Matsyendrasana (the Spinal Twist) in that order in order to ensure a correct sequence of backward and forward bending of the spine. Each asana should be repeated three times. For a shorter sitting, Paschimottanasana, Chakrasana, Matsyasana, and Yoga Mudra may be dispensed with. The Shirshasana head stand relieves pressure on the lumbar and sacral regions of the vertebral column.

As far as Qi Gong is concerned, the Ba Duan Jin Eight Pieces of Brocade arm stretching exercises (Exercises 2, 5, and 6 on pages 112-115) are particularly useful for strengthening the back. The Nei Dan Xiao Zhou Tian, or Small Circulation technique, in the seated pose should be practiced daily. Also of benefit, for those with less time to spare, is ten minutes a day of deep breathing in the Qi Gong standing pose with knees slightly bent and arms outstretched as if to hold a balloon (see page 92 or 128).

PREMENSTRUAL SYNDROME

By some calculations over 50 percent of all women suffer from varying degrees of premenstrual syndrome (PMS). In its mildest form PMS gives rise to slight discomfort and irritability about one week to ten days before the onset of menstruation. At its worst PMS can be characterized by depression, abdominal cramps, headaches, pains all over the body, fainting, anger, violence, and thoughts of suicide. The basic cause is hormonal imbalance although low blood sugar, allergies, and stress can make it worse.

The Qi Gong/Pranayama remedy is to counteract the imbalance with endorphins. These are manufactured by the body during deep breathing exercise and have the effect of boosting mood and giving a "natural high."

Exercises which have a toning up effect on the internal organs of reproduction might offer some relief. These exercises are: abdominal breathing in general, be it Pranayama or Qi Gong, Kapalabhati, Uddiyana Bandha, Bhujangasana (the Cobra), Halasana (the Plow), Dhanurasana (the Bow), Ardha-Matsyendrasana (the Spinal Twist), Yoga Mudra (the Symbol of Yoga) and Ekpada Uttanasana (single leg raising) also have a general toning effect with specific emphasis on the abdominal area (see chapter 7 for further details).

SEXUAL PROBLEMS: See Uro-Genital Problems

SINUSITIS

Sinusitis is an inflammation of the nasal tissues. It may be due to hay fever, irritant fumes, or a cold. Chronic sinusitis may be caused by injury or a growth in the nasal passage.

The treatment, in all cases, is to remove the underlying cause. Get away from the smoke or fumes, remove the growth, or cure the cold.

Pranayama and Qi Gong are of no avail until the nasal passage is free and you are able to breath normally. Sutraneti and Jalaneti with warm salty water have been known to help.

See Allergic Rhinitis for Jalaneti variations in cases of allergic sinusitis.

SMOKING DEPENDENCY: See Drug Dependency

STRESS

Stress is part of life. The very process of being alive means dealing with sensory messages bombarding people from all directions, all the time. Responding to these stimuli—earning a living, driving, making love, worrying about the future—puts stress on people's nervous systems and bodies. Luckily, the healthy nervous system is like a dynamo: set it reacting to a certain level of stress and not only will it continue responding, it will come to demand stress in order to feel alive.[7]

It is only when the stimuli are overwhelming that people begin to suffer. The cause of distress may be prolonged unwelcome situations (unpleasant work conditions, poverty, an abusive relationship), or it may be due to illness or a series of disasters such as a death, or loss of one's job or home. When stress becomes distress, it can lead to insomnia, hair loss, irritability, fatigue, indigestion, headaches, and a weakened immune system. One would hope to be able to intervene before coming down with a full-blown illness.

The universal strategy for dealing with stress is to breathe deeply and to relax. Hobbies, interests, new activities, laughter, and falling in love will all help. It is, however, the ancient and universal remedy of deep breathing taken to level of a science that will afford the greatest and longest lasting relief. Pranayama and Qi Gong breathing exercises the lungs, improves the metabolism, and calms the nerves. Any Pranayama and yoga program (see chapter 6) or Nei Dan and Wai Dan Qi Gong exercises practiced regularly, every day, are useful in combating stress. The importance of regularity cannot be overemphasized. For those moments when stress is getting the better of you, try sitting down to five minutes Pranayama, or Qi Gong, abdominal deep breathing without kumbhaka breath retention. This can be done anywhere—at the factory or office, during surgery, or in a plane or car— without attracting undue attention to yourself.

For a full program of exercises see Anxiety and Instability.

ULCERS: See Gastric And Peptic Ulcers

URO-GENITAL PROBLEMS

Displaced Uterus

The uterus may become displaced during a difficult childbirth.

The most effective remedy is regular Pranayama with kumbhaka breath retention and bandhas. Gomukhasana (the Cow posture), Yoga Mudra, Paschimottanasana (the forward stretch), and Matsyasana (the Fish) should follow.

Frigidity

The inability to experience sexual pleasure is usually due to underlying psychological problems stemming from fear, guilt, memories of sexual abuse, or feelings of inadequacy. Occasionally the cause is physiological: an inadequate lubrication of the vagina, for example, which may, in turn, be due to hormonal imbalances or vitamin deficiencies.

When inability to experience sexual pleasure is due to hormonal imbalance, Qi Gong and Pranayama may help. Pranayama and Qi Gong exercises are known to exert a beneficial effect on the internal organs and on the endocrine system.

When psychological problems are responsible for lack of interest in sex, the best therapy short of falling passionately in love with the perfect man or woman is to practice Pranayama and Qi Gong breathing followed by fifteen or twenty minutes of relaxation in the Shavasana lying position.

While relaxing it may help to focus, and perhaps fantasize, on sexual themes. Often an alert mind in a relaxed body can cast light on, and come to terms with, many of the barely conscious problems and processes of the psyche. As a matter of interest, Tantric adepts are in the habit of visualizing copulation between themselves and a deity of their choice as a means of rendering sex "sacred" and free of "low" carnal desire. A similar technique might be employed to render sex free from fear or guilt.

Salutary asanas for toning up the organs involved in sex are: Halasana (the Plow—see page 76), Bhujangasana (the Cobra—see page 77), Ardha-Matsyendrasana (the Spinal Twist—see page 80) and Yoga Mudra (see page 82).

Wai Dan Qi Gong followed by self massage can also help.

Menstrual Problems

Irregularities in the menstrual cycle as well as menstrual cramps and excessive or prolonged loss of blood can all depend on hormonal or emotional imbalances.

When this is the cause, yoga, Pranayama, and Qi Gong may all be useful in correcting the underlying imbalance.

Before embarking on breathing therapy one should, of course, seek medical advice to ensure that the problems are not due to disease or other deficiencies. Once ensured, the following exercises should be practiced:

Kapalabhati or Bhastrika followed by alternate nostril Pranayama with kumbhaka breath retention in either the Jalandhara or the Mula Bandha: twenty rounds a day. Halasana (the Plow), Dhanurasana (the Bow), Ardha-Matsyendrasana (the Spinal Twist), Yoga Mudra, and Ekpada Uttanasana (single leg raising) are all indicated for relieving menstrual problems. Bhujangasana (the Cobra) is especially effective for relieving irregularities in the menstrual cycle and correcting utero-overine troubles. Please refer to chapter 7 for information on how to do these asanas.

Sexual Weakness

Although a few sexual problems such as impotence may have an anatomical base, most are entirely psychological in origin. Premature ejaculation, nonphysiological impotence, and frigidity can thus be treated effectively through Prana and Qi control.

Often enough, the main cause of the problem is psychological tension. To counteract it, any form of Pranayama or Qi Gong can be employed. One should learn to circulate energy by means of Nei Dan, to observe and to control the emotions through alternate nostril breathing and kumbhaka breath retention, and to work off tension through Wai Dan or Hatha yoga exercises. Yoga Mudra is said to be particularly effective.

One must learn, in short, to control and come to terms with one's physical energy, including the sexual aspect of it.

If premature ejaculation is the problem, controlled deep abdominal breathing during lovemaking should help. When the urge to ejaculate becomes overpowering, kumbhaka breath retention may be resorted to in a last ditch effort to check it. Holding the breath will distract momentarily from the excitement in hand and will reestablish some measure of control over the emotions.

For preventive therapy, Qi Gong has the following exercise to offer:

Lie down in bed with a thick pillow behind your neck. Concentrate on the Dan Tian four inches below your navel and massage your abdominal area as follows:

Place your left palm flat against your navel with your right palm over your left hand. Beginning with an upward movement from left to right, make thirty-six circles around your navel with your palms. Now place your right palm against your abdomen with the left hand over the top. Make thirty-six circles in the opposite direction.

The second stage of the exercise is to place your palms flat against your abdomen with your thumbs touching the rib cage. The fingers of your hands should point to one another at about six inches apart. Rub your fingers vertically down across your abdomen to your groin. Reverse the motion and bring your hands back up to your ribs. This movement should be repeated thirty-six times at a rate of one stroke a second. On the downward stroke, pressure should be on your thumbs, on the upward stroke, on your little fingers.

Daily practice is supposed to assure a definite cure against premature ejaculation. If your partner is still awake when you are through, you can find out.

VARICOSE VEINS

Swollen veins due to blood congestion are a common ailment which leads to thickening of the limbs and to much discomfort. Varicose veins usually occur in the legs. They are normally due to malfunctioning valves in the veins which fail to prevent blood from reversing its flow and, by so doing, allow it to stagnate in the afflicted limb instead of circulating upward through the rest of the body. Varicose veins are made worse by lack of exercise, obesity, and too much standing. The usual treatment, short of surgery, is to wear an elastic bandage over the affected area.

Pranayama and Qi Gong afford relief by promoting better blood circulation. When a sitting posture is adopted during breathing exercises, pressure is exerted directly on the congested veins thus diminishing discomfort in the limbs.

Any postures which force the blood away from the congested areas by force of gravity are similarly effective. One should therefore practice the Shirshasana head stand and the Sarvangasana candle posture whenever possible.

VERTIGO

Vertigo refers to a sense of dizziness and poor sense of balance. The causes may be psychological (as for example a fear of heights), high or low blood pressure, allergy, anemia, head or brain injuries or tumors, neurological problems, middle ear infections, or blockages or lack of oxygen to the brain. The physical cause must always be found and treated first. If the vertigo subsists, or is due to poor blood circulation to the brain, Pranayama, yoga, and Qi Gong can help.

A Pranayama breathing program starting with Kapalabhati and ending with Ujjayi helps improve circulation and consequently the flow of blood to the brain. Yoga postures such as the Sarvangasana shoulder stand and the Shirshasana head stand are specific in bringing blood to the head by force of gravity; both also enhance the sense of balance.

A Qi Gong program of deep Nei Dan breathing (see page 94) followed by a head and face massage (see pages 99-100) is also valid.

Notes

INTRODUCTION

1. Tai Chi Chuan (Tai Ji Quan) is, in effect, a martial art that comes under the general heading of Qi Gong.

CHAPTER 1

1. *Bhagavadgita*, Book 5, verses, 27-28.

2. The *Yogasutras*, I, verses 2-3.

3. The *Yogasutras*, I, verses 33-34.

4. The *Yogasutras*, I, verses 49-53.

5. *Brihadyogiyajnavalkyasmrti*, Chapter 8, verses 12-13.

6. *Brihadyogiyajnavalkyasmrti*, Chapter 8, verses 26-40.

7. *Brihadyogiyajnavalkyasmrti,* Chapter 8, verses 38-40.

8. *Hathapradipika*, Lesson 1, verse 49.

9. Needham, Joseph. *Science and Civilization in China*, Vol. 2 (Cambridge University Press, 1956), 144.

10. Huang-Di Nei-Jing, Plain Questions, *Inner Classic of the Yellow Emperor* ascribed to Emperor Huang Di (2698-2589 B.C.), but actually compiled by various unknown authors during the Warring States period (475-221 B.C.).

11. Needham, Joseph. *Science and Civilization in China*, Vol. 2, 143.

12. Traditional Chinese saying, possibly from Warring States period (475-221 B.C.).

13. I use the term "may have" because there is evidence to suggest that it might have been the other way around. Taoist sexual practices may have been exported into India where they gave rise to Tantric yoga. In fact, Tantric yoga was most popular in those regions of India that were most susceptible to influence from China: Assam and the North East. Chinese Tantric Buddhism would thus owe more to native Taoism than to anything Indian.

14. Needham, Joseph. *Science and Civilization in China*, Vol. 2, 429.

CHAPTER 2

1. Swami Kuvalayananda. *Pranayama* (Lonavla: Kaivalyadhama Publishers, 1931).

CHAPTER 3

1. *Gheranda Samhita*, Lesson 5, verses 5-7.

2. *Hathapradipika*, Lesson 1, verse 12.

3. *Hathapradipika*, Lesson 1, verse 63.
4. *Hathapradipika*, Lesson 1, verse 62.
5. *Hathapradipika*, Lesson 1, verse 63.

CHAPTER 4
1. *Hathapradipika*, Lesson 3, verse 69.

CHAPTER 5
1. Pratap, Dr. Yoga Mimamsa newsletter (Lonavla, India: the Kaivalyadhama Institute, August, 1969).
2. *Hathapradipika*, Lesson 2, verses 60-65.
3. *Gheranda Samhita*, Lesson 5, verse 71.
4. *Gheranda Samhita*, Lesson 5, verse 72.
5. *Hathapradipika*, Lesson 2, verse 65.
6. *Gheranda Samhita*, Lesson 2, verses 66-67.
7. *Gheranda Samhita*, Lesson 5, verse 59.
8. *Hathapradipika*, Lesson 2, verse 50.
9. *Gheranda Samhita*, Lesson 5, verse 63.
10. *Hathapradipika*, Lesson 2, verse 68.
11. *Hathapradipika*, Lesson 2, verse 58.
12. *Hathapradipika*, Lesson 5, verses 54-56.
13. *Hathapradipika*, Lesson 2, verse 69.
14. *Hathapradipika*, Lesson 5, verse 70.
15. *Hathapradipika*, Lesson 2, verse 64.
16. *Gheranda Samhita*, Lesson 1, verse 21. To perform Bahiskrita dhauti, one is told to "retain the air in the stomach for one and a half hours and force it down along the lower passage. Standing navel-deep in water, one should then push out the rectum and wash it with one's hands until all the fecal matter has been removed. Having washed the rectum clean, one should draw it back into the abdomen." Intriguing, perhaps, but not something to be emulated. Although this exercise may be physically possible, there exists no authentic report on it ever having been demonstrated.
17. *Omni Longevity Magazine*, V. 1, no. 3, December 1988.

CHAPTER 11
1. *Chandamaharosana Tantra*, Tibetan fifteenth century A.D. text.

CHAPTER 12
1. Nineteenth century Chinese proverb.
2. The author's sources are the 1987 publications of the Chinese Qi Gong Scientific Research Institute.
3. The Kaivalyadhama Yoga Research Institute in Lonavla, India, and the Indian Institute of Yoga in Patna, India.
4. *Hathapradipika*, Lesson 5, verse 22.
5. Joshi, K. S., M.D. "Treatment of Insomnia through Yoga and Nature Cure Techniques." *Yoga Awareness Journal*, Volume IV, number 3, August 1980, India.
6. A Vajrayana (Tibetan) Buddhist saying, which I paraphrased has been quoted by many, including the Tibetan Buddhist leader, the Dalai Lama: "An action oft repeated becomes a habit, a habit in time becomes a personality, a personality carried through life becomes a destiny."
7. Sensory deprivation experiments show that, when starved of all ordinary stimuli of sight, sound, smell, or touch, subjects very soon begin manufacturing a hallucinatory world of their own.

Index

Jivha Bandha, 47
Jnana-Mudra, 42
Joints, 35-38
   pains, 49

K
Kaivalyadhama Yoga Research Institute, vi, 22, 52, 67, 163, 164
Kapalabhati, 53
Ke Chi, snapping teeth, 102
Knees, 38, 103
Krishna, Swami, 140
Kumbhaka, 43
   holding breath out, 53
Kundalini, 4, 20, 39, 46, 59, 134
Kung Fu, see Gong Fu
Kuvalayananda, Swami, vi, 22, 63

L
Lao Tzu, 10
Laying on of hands, 22
Legs, numbness, 50
Lian Qi—training the Qi, 97
Ligaments, 38, 80
Liu Han Min, 146
Liu He Ba Fa technique, 16
Locust position, see Shalabhasana
Loosening up exercises, 99
Loss of awareness breath, see Moorcha
Lou, minor Qi channels, 22
Lumbago, 80, 103
Lumbar massage, 103
Luoyang, 10
Lying position for Qi Gong, 93, 129

M
Marijuana, 157
Martial arts, 16, 20, 97
Massage, 99, 177
Matra, 5
Matsyasana—the Fish, 74
Mayol, Jaques, 29
Meals and breathing exercises, 30
Medicine, Western, 137
Mencius, or Meng-Tzu, 13
Menstrual problems, 176
Migraine, 164
Ming Gu drumming, 100
Moksha, 52
Moorcha, or loss of awareness breath, 61
Mouth, breathing through, 60, 61
Mudra, hand positions, 42, 52
Mula Bandha, 46
Multiple sclerosis, 168
Music, 71

N
Nadis, 6, 44
Nan Jing (classic on disorders), 9
Nasal cleansing, 27-28
Nasal cleansing breath, see Bhastrika
Needham, Prof. J., 7
Nei Dan, 11, 15, 16, 94
Nei Dan Grand Circulation or Da Zhou Tian, 96
Nei Dan Qi Gong Small Circulation or Xiao Zhou Tian, 94
Neurasthenia, 170
Numbness in the legs, 50

O
Obesity, 171
Orgasm, 5, 14, 134, 135
Osteoarthritis, 145
Oxidization, 21, 54
Oxygen, 21, 22, 62, 137
   consumption, 21, 30, 53

P
Padmasambhava, 14
Padmasana or the Lotus, 36
Paschimottanasana forward stretch, 81
Patanjali's Yogasutras, 3, 4
Pauling, Linus, 141
Pawanmuktasana—Wind Liberating position, 87
Peptic ulcers, 161
Perineum, 38
Perseverance, importance of, 20, 32, 51
Personality disorders, 172
Philtrum, 101
Plavini or floating breath, 62
Plow posture, see Halasana
Pneuma, 1, 15
Position for breathing exercise, 35
Postural defects, 173
Pranayama
   and Hatha yoga, 20, 67
   and Qi Gong compared, 15, 19
   definition of, 2
Pratap, Dr., 52
Premenstrual syndrome (PMS), 173
Prickly sensations, 50
Programs, 65
Puraka, or inhalation, 42

Q
Qi
   channels, 20, 22, 91, 104
   defined, 8
Qi Gong
   and Pranayama compared, 15, 19
   definition of, 8
   in a hurry, 127
   origin of, 8
   today, 17
Qi Gong Scientific Research Institute, 137

R
Ramakrishna, 20
Rapid heartbeat, 49
Rechaka or exhalation, 43
Regularity of practice, 20, 32, 51
Ren Mei channel, 91, 95
Reproduction, 134
   organs of, 176
Reverse breathing, 94
Rheumatism, 125
Rheumatoid arthritis, 145
Rimpoche, Guru, 14
Rishikesh, 140

S
Sakta, 4, 135
Samadhi, 3, 21
Sarvangasana—the Candle Stand, 73
Schizophrenia, 172